FALLING FOR THE BROKEN

S. N. CHRISTENSEN

CONTENTS

DEDICATION

For everyone who hides their pain behind a smile while quietly breaking inside. For those who pretend to be fine for the world, carrying loneliness in silence–may these pages remind you that you are never truly alone.

$$\bullet \ \bullet \ \bullet \ \bullet \ \bullet \ \bullet \ \bullet \ \bullet \ \bullet \ \bullet$$

AUTHOR'S NOTES

This book can be read as a standalone in the fALLINg series and ends with a HEA. If you plan on reading the first four in the series, I suggest you read those first to avoid spoilers about other characters.

Some content in this book may be triggering to some readers. Trigger Warnings include mention of suicide, overdosing, mention of kidnapping, violence, and the use of drugs and alcohol.

If you are having thoughts of harming yourself, please know you are not alone, and help is available. If you are in immediate danger, call your local emergency number (for example, 911 in the U.S.). In the United States and its territories, you can call or text **988** for the Suicide & Crisis Lifeline; you can also text **HOME** to **741741** for the Crisis Text Line. If you're elsewhere, please reach out to local emergency services or a trusted person.

CHAPTER ONE

JAKE

The air hangs heavy with the smell of stale beer and despair. Depressed drunks are crawling all over the bar tonight, me being one of them. It's been a while since I've found myself sulking on Valentine's Day. It's not typically a day I even care about or acknowledge its existence. However, this one is different.

Pushing my glass toward the bartender, he passes by and takes it. I don't need to ask for a refill before he tosses another at me. The benefits of being friends with the owner, free drinks. I only have a few twenties left to my name, and they're all currently sitting in my wallet. I should be thinking about where I'm going to sleep tonight, but instead I'm enjoying drowning my sorrows with alcohol.

As if I have some sort of communal disease, the seats next to me have stayed empty, until now. Someone plops into the seat to my left and flags down the bartender. The way he's wobbling indicates he's already drunk. I don't fully look over because I'm not in the mood for any more small talk. I had enough of that earlier in the day.

He shifts in his seat before I hear the sharp clunk of his drink hitting the counter. "Jake?! Is that you, man?"

Ah, shit. Looking over toward the disheveled man, I'm not at all surprised to see him in this state. I probably look similar to him.

I force a smile and give a quick pat on his back, letting out an exaggerated exclamation. "Eric, my man!"

The poor guy looks like he hasn't shaved, slept, or sobered up in over a week. His blue eyes are glassy and unfocused, like maybe booze wasn't the only thing he got into tonight. His brown hair is a shaggy, unkempt mess, with the black-rimmed glasses sliding crookedly down his nose. He looks like hell. Honestly, I can't blame him.

"What are you doing here? Shouldn't you be celebrating with your bestie?" he asks, sounding surprisingly coherent.

"I skipped out a little early, but I'm sure they're already on their way to the honeymoon," I answer with a shrug.

He looks me over like he's trying to read me. I'm curious about what conclusion he's coming to. I know that I'm a mess as I've had too many drinks, and I'm pretty sure I've been ripping the hair out of my head for the past hour. Do I even have any left?

I don't have to wait long for him to tell me what he thinks. "You loved her too, huh? I always had a feeling. I'm sorry. I bet you secretly hated me."

"Nah, you were good to her," I say.

Maybe that's a little bit of a lie. Not the being good to her part though, because he was great for her. He was everything that she needed at the time. I didn't like him for a while because he's right. I was in love with her, or so I thought. I'm not even sure anymore.

Tonight, I'm not getting drunk only because my best friend, the girl I was pining after for years, got married. I probably would've been a little depressed about that, but a couple of beers would've sufficed. No, my father had to cut me off on the same day. What a shitty Valentine's Day this has turned out to be. Not to mention, it's my birthday.

"Well, here's to us losers who lost an amazing girl," he says while clinking his glass to mine.

He's not wrong. Everly really is amazing. Our only problem and why we couldn't keep her is because we weren't James. I never thought I believed much in fate or soul mates, but damn if I can deny that they were meant to be together.

"So, what are you doing after this?" he asks.

I'm not really in the mood for small talk, but he's the closest thing I have to a friend right now. He's a cool guy, so why not?

"Well, I'm going to find a bench to sleep on and figure out what I'm going to do with my life when I get sober. My dad cut me off, which means he locked me out of my apartment, froze all my accounts, and basically disowned me," I say, like it's just a normal day in my life.

"Oh man, really? What did you do to deserve that?"

Honestly, I don't know. I thought things were going fine, but he didn't think so. Yeah, I might have been partying a little too much, but I got business done. My image didn't look the best, but the tabloids portrayed me however they wanted to. I'm not the same as I was back in college, but my father doesn't believe that. I wasn't even bad back then, but people always see what they want to see.

"I don't represent his company the way he wants me to. It's probably best this way. My brother was smart and had no interest in taking over the business," I respond.

Bash is the smarter brother. He's two and a half years older than I am. He always knew what he wanted to do with his life, and that was not taking over my father's company. I wanted to be a good son and follow in my father's footsteps, but he never seemed to care much for me. I was always disappointing him with whatever I did, so I never corrected him when he thought I was being stupid. Yeah, I had some fun, but it was nowhere near what he thought I was doing.

"What about your friends or brother? Can't you stay with them?" he asks.

"No," I state, not wanting to elaborate.

Yeah, Bash would force me to move in with him if he found out I was completely cut off and had no place to stay, but I don't want to do that. For one, he's asking his girlfriend to move in. And honestly, I just don't want to depend on my brother or anyone. Even Ben, my best friend, would help if I asked, but I'd rather figure things out on my own. This is my problem to fix, and honestly, I'm embarrassed.

"Shit, well, I have a spare bedroom. Come stay with me as long as you want. I'm rarely home since I work late hours," he says sincerely.

I give him a half-smile. "I appreciate the offer, but I'll figure it out."

He shakes his head. "No, I'm serious. I can't let you stay on the streets when I have a room that's never used. Just stay until you figure things out. Honestly, it gets kind of lonely. I haven't really made any friends yet."

Looking in his eyes, he looks pathetic. He looks sad. Is losing Everly really what did this to him? They were together for about two years and engaged to be married. He was always a positive and happy guy. Once she broke it off with him, I know he worked his butt off to move across the country to try to win her back. She shot him down during their first meeting and, being the nice guy he is, he left her alone.

We got along fine when we all hung out together, and he seems to really need a friend right now. Who am I to deny his request?

"Yeah, okay. Thanks."

"Really? Alright, whenever you're ready, we can head back to my place. I have a spare key I can give you. Do you have any stuff?" He asks, looking a little happier now.

"Just what I've got in this bag. My father was kind enough to let me take a few personal items from my apartment," I say.

We both finish up our drinks, throw a tip on the bar, and I say a quick thanks to my buddy for the drinks. We head out and walk down the street a couple of blocks to his apartment. It's not what I'm used to, but it looks decent. At least it's not super run-down. Eric is a smart guy. I know he makes decent money in the city. Just not the kind of money I'm used to.

We walk into his place, and it's basically empty. He has a couch and a TV in the living room. The counter in the kitchen has nothing on it other than a toaster. I'm pretty sure that if I look in his cabinets, there will only be a few plates and cups. There's a two-person table in the kitchenette area, and the walls are completely bare.

He leads me to my room, where a made bed and dresser wait for me. I throw my bag on the bed and leave it there as he shows me the bathroom just outside my door. He has his own bathroom attached to his room, so he says this one is all mine.

The place is honestly depressing. There's nothing but the basics here and no décor, not even a single picture frame. How does he live like this?

"It's not much, but it does its job. I really am rarely here, so make yourself at home. Stay as long as you need," he says, rummaging through a drawer.

"Thanks, I owe you one once I get my life together," I reply, sitting down on the couch.

He comes over and hands me a key. I go to take my keys out of my pocket but remember I don't have any. Opening my wallet, I stick it in there. My father also took my car. Honestly, I could have fought him for some of this stuff, considering how many years I worked for him and made my own money, but it wasn't worth it to me. I don't want anything to do with him or his money right now.

Eric disappears into his room to pass out, and I decide that's not a bad idea. After a quick shower, I head to my own room and dig through my duffel bag for a charger, only to remember I don't even have a phone anymore. I'm not sure if my father disconnected it, but I left it behind in my apartment, along with everything else I didn't want. Instead of spiraling over the mess that is my life, I stretch out on my temporary bed and let sleep take me.

Chapter Two

Jake

Walking the streets of New York City isn't what it's cracked up to be. It's busy, loud, and exhausting. Taking the subway is even worse. I never considered myself one of those snobby rich kids, but right now I'm feeling like one. My anxiety is through the roof, and I miss my car. Okay, it's not my car that I miss... it's my driver. I can't believe I took Stan for granted for so many years. If I ever see him again, I'm going to lay a big fat kiss on his cheek and give him a raise. That man deserves a raise.

I shake my head, trying to push thoughts of the past away. It's depressing to realize I'll probably never have that again. Tempting as it is to show up at my brother's door and ask for help, I can't. Instead, I'm heading to an old friend, asking for a favor.

It only took a day to figure out my next step. Borrowing some of Eric's clothes was easy since we're about the same size, and the guy owns more suits than he'll ever need. Using his phone, a quick call to my buddy Tristan landed me a job. He didn't even ask questions, just told me to come in Monday to talk about the position.

So here I am, taking the subway and walking to my new employer, the place I'll be working for the foreseeable future. As I'm heading up the stairs from the subway, a woman catches my attention as she trips on a step and drops her bag, spilling all its contents and papers. Everyone is sidestepping her as she picks herself up, rubs her hand over her face, and groans.

I quicken my pace to reach her, helping grab the papers and other items that tumbled from her bag. Together, we climb the remaining steps and move to the side, out of everyone's way.

"Thanks," she says, as I hand her everything I picked up.

"You're welcome," I reply, about to walk away until I notice she's crying.

Crap. I don't have time for this. How can I leave her like this, though? I take a quick look, and she's... cute. Her dark brown hair is pulled up into a bun, and she has beautiful blue eyes. She looks like she is either coming or going from work as she has on a navy-blue suit.

"Are you okay?" I ask gently.

She wipes away the tears on her face and looks at the sky, sighing. "It's been a shitty day..." she pauses to laugh, "who am I kidding? It's been a shitty month."

I nod and force a smile. "I feel that."

"Thank you again for your help. I didn't mean to waste any of your time," she states as if she's not worthy of someone helping her.

I look her over, and there's something about her that seems familiar. I don't think I've ever met her before. If I had, she would've said something by now. Maybe it's just the sadness in her eyes. She's smiling now, but I can tell she's just hiding her true feelings behind it.

"Where are you heading? Can I help you carry your bag?" I ask because I noticed her favoring one leg as she stands.

Her eyes go wide. "Oh, no. I can manage. It's not that heavy."

I laugh. "Seriously, I don't mind. It looks like you hurt your leg."

She looks down and shakes her head. "I did that a bit ago. It still gives me some trouble, mainly on stairs."

She looks me up and down like she's trying to figure something out. Maybe I look familiar to her too? Well, either way, she clearly doesn't need my help anymore, so I need to get going.

"Well, if you're sure you're okay, I'm going to head out," I say, gesturing over my shoulder toward the path I'm taking.

She nods, so I walk off. I take only three steps before she stops me. "Wait."

Turning around, I wait for her to continue. She looks nervous. "Do you... do you happen to know anywhere that's hiring?"

I cock my head and look her over again. She seems nice enough, and she's dressed professionally for an interview.

Would it hurt to bring her to meet Tristan too? Being that he owns a hotel, I'm sure he has some openings that she may be good for.

I grin. "Yeah, actually, I do. I'm heading to talk with my buddy about a job now if you want to come with me."

Her face lights up. "Really?"

I nod. "He owns a hotel down the street."

She rushes up beside me and starts rambling. "That's amazing. I really appreciate it. You don't have to vouch for me or anything. I have my resume here and everything. I just got turned down for a job that I've been interviewing for and really need one before I get evicted from my apartment..." she stops talking abruptly before continuing, "I'm sorry... I... You didn't need to know any of that."

I laugh and shake my head. "Nah, you can tell me anything. Sometimes it helps to get things off your chest. It does sound like you've had a bad go of it."

She clears her throat. "Yeah, I have..."

We're silent for the rest of the walk to Tristan's hotel. She looked like she was on the verge of tears a few times on the walk but kept pushing it down. Now, before entering, she just looks nervous.

I put my arm out to stop her. "So, there's one important thing I need to know before we go in."

She looks at me worried. "What is it?"

I smile. "Your name."

She relaxes and smiles back. Her smile is beautiful, but I can tell there is so much more behind it she doesn't let people see.

"Jules, short for Juliet," she responds.

"Jules…" I repeat. "I'm Jake, short for Jacob."

She holds out her hand for me to shake. "Nice to meet you, Jake. Thank you again for this."

"No problem," I say, opening the door for her.

We make our way to the check-in desk, and while waiting in line, I take in the lobby. Fancy, just as I expected. He owns a string of five-star hotels around the world, which rivals my father's. A large chandelier hangs overhead, marble floors stretch across the space, and a sleek seating area with a fireplace and modern furniture invites guests to sit.

The man behind the desk calls me forward. Jules stays beside me the whole time.

"Hey Jack," I say in a friendly tone as I read his nametag. "I'm here to see Mr. Mercer."

He nods and types something into his computer. "What's your name?"

"Jacob Hale," I state.

He continues typing and then uses the phone to call someone. After a few sentences are exchanged, he sends me up the elevator a floor and down toward an office where his secretary meets me.

Her face is plastered with a fake smile as she greets us. "Mr. Hale! It's so great to finally meet you."

I nod and give her a fake smile back. Clearly, she thinks it's genuine, which I can tell because she's checking me out. Not interested, Tonya.

"You too," I say, hoping she'll get on with letting me see Tristan.

Her smile drops when she looks over at Jules. "I wasn't aware anyone else would be with you."

I lean forward on her desk, getting closer and turning up my charm. "Ah, she's someone I wanted Mr. Mercer to meet."

She blushes due to our proximity and clears her throat. "Of course. May I get her name?"

Jules steps forward to answer. "It's Jules..."

"Jake!" Tristan calls as he comes out of his office and heads my way.

"Tristan, my man! Long time no see," I greet, patting him on the shoulder.

"You look the same as the last time I saw you back in college. How are you?" he asks.

I laugh. "Great, besides the fact that I'm here."

He shakes his head. "I have no idea the circumstances, but you know I have your back..."

He trails off when he finally notices Jules behind me, and his smile grows. She's gorgeous, and he's clearly checking her out. I don't know why, but that makes me angry. I don't want him to look at her like that.

He looks between us, and his grin widens. "Ah, I get it now. I get it. What's her name?"

Usually, I wouldn't like that he's talking to me about someone when they're in the room versus addressing them, but I don't want him around her more than necessary. He's the definition of a playboy. At least he was back in our college days.

"This is Jules. She's also in need of a job," I state, not clarifying that I just met her on the street less than an hour ago.

He laughs. "I was right. I see what's going on. You fell in love, and the old man didn't approve, so he gave an ultimatum."

It takes a moment to comprehend what he's saying, and I don't have any time to correct it before he continues. "Yeah, sure. We can find a job for her."

He looks toward her and says, "Give Tonya your information, and I'll be out after I talk to Jake."

Jules nods and says, "Thank you so much."

I follow Tristan into his office, and we both sit at his desk. I feel out of place here. Not only because it's a big competition to my company, or should I say, my father's company, but because I'm needing a job. I'm used to being the acting boss, not someone who has nothing to his name and begs for a job.

"So, tell me what's going on," Tristan finally states.

I knew this was coming. I keep my answer vague, especially now that he thinks Jules and I are together. I should set the record straight, but I don't. For some reason, I like the idea of him believing she's mine.

I shrug my shoulders. "You know my old man. He didn't approve of the decisions I've made, so he kicked me to the curb. I'm living with a friend and have nothing to my name."

He whistles. "Wow, that's rough. My dad gets on my case a lot, but I can't imagine him doing anything like that. I've got your back, though. I could use your expertise."

I shake my head. "I appreciate it, but I just want something simple to get back on my feet. Put me at the front desk or something to check in guests."

He laughs until he sees I'm serious. "Jake… you've basically run your own hotel chain. I could use you up here with me…" he pauses to look me over. "Unless you're thinking about heading back to your father's company?"

I think about that for a moment. Do I plan to head back to work for my father? The other day, that would've been an immediate no. I was pissed off at him and never wanted anything to do with him again. But now I've had time to calm down. I haven't put much thought into it, but I know deep down I still want my father's approval. I want to be good enough for him. I want to show him that I'm not worthless, like he thinks I am.

I shake my head. "I don't have plans to go back, but he's family, you know?"

He leans forward with his elbow on his desk and chin in his hand. "Yeah, I know. Then I need you to be straight with me. You're not going to screw me over in the end, are you?"

I squeeze my brows together and stare at him before responding. "Of course not. You don't really think I'd do that, do you?"

He slaps the desk and lets out a sigh of relief. "Nah, I don't. Just had to ask. Well, whatever job you want, it's yours. I'd like you up here, but if you insist on starting from the bottom up, I need a new housekeeping manager."

It takes everything in me not to let out a groan and keep the smile on my face. "Are you sure you don't have room for my friendly personality at your front desk?"

He grins. "Nope, but if you get sick of that role, let me know. We can bring you on board to help us here."

I shake my head. I really don't want to get involved with his hotel like that. Not that I wouldn't love to do it, but like he said, I'm not positive if I'm going back to my father's or not.

"Housekeeping manager sounds great then, but you know you can ask me for help with anything. I really appreciate you doing this for me," I say.

"No problem," he says as we both stand and head toward the door.

"I'll give your girlfriend a job in housekeeping as well, but I expect that you two will keep things professional while at work," he says, winking.

I laugh. "Of course."

I exit his office and sit in the chair next to Tonya's desk as Jules heads in next. I hope she doesn't give away that he misread our relationship and how we know each other. I have no idea why I didn't tell him the truth, but it's too late now.

Chapter Three

JULES

Well, that was not how I saw today going. I woke up this morning thinking I was going to get a job as a dance instructor, not a housekeeper at a hotel. Not to mention now having a fake boyfriend. What has my life turned into?

My phone rings, breaking me from my thoughts. I groan as I see my brother calling and hit ignore, just like I've done every time he calls lately.

Not even a minute later, a text comes through.

Bro

> Jules I haven't seen you in two months.
> Call me.

My heart sinks with guilt. Has it really been two months? Two long months since I lost my dream job. Two months of everything unraveling, all because of one stupid mistake on the dance floor.

I shake my head to keep those depressing thoughts from crowding my mind again. I send back a quick text.

Sorry I promise I'll call soon. Super busy!

Lies, lies and more lies. I'm not planning on calling anytime soon. I'm not super busy. I'm just a crappy sister who can't find the courage to tell her brother that she's a loser and will never amount to anything in life.

Okay, maybe I am a little harsh on myself, but it's true. I trained all my life to be on Broadway in New York. My parents spent more money than they had on dance and singing lessons for me. My brother was put on the back burner, but he never once resented me for it. He was always my biggest supporter and still is.

So yeah, I feel like a crappy sister right now. He's been going through a lot, and I can't even find the time to talk or see him. I just know that I won't be able to hide my current situation from him. Which means he'll do everything he can to help me, and I don't want that. I'm also not ready to have the conversation about my career being over.

My phone buzzes with another text.

> No. We're going out to dinner. Tell me
> what day you're free. Mom and dad said
> you're avoiding them too.

Ugh. I knew he would eventually push me for this. We have been getting together once a week since he moved to New York. He knows something is going on. He's also right that I've been avoiding our parents. Thankfully, they still live in Georgia, so I just keep to texting them simple messages as well.

> I'll get back to you. I'm working odd and late hours!

That's not entirely a lie. I will be working odd hours as a housekeeper. I shake my head and throw my phone on my bed. I need to prepare for my first day at work tomorrow. I don't know the first thing about being a housekeeper, but I figure Google will help. How hard can it be?

I've officially gone down the rabbit hole of Google. Three hours later, I feel sick to my stomach. I found one thread about housekeeping horror stories and then I just kept going. Why did I keep going? The number of things people have seen while cleaning hotel rooms is crazy. I have a new appreciation for those who come in to clean after me in hotels.

Getting ready for bed, I unwrap my knee and ankle since sleeping with them wrapped feels uncomfortable. The air helps, and being a deep sleeper means I barely move, anyway. Stretching out on the mattress, a sigh of relief slips out. It's been a long day, and even though the job I wanted didn't work out, at least there's one waiting and no eviction notice coming.

I close my eyes and there he is, Jake, the stranger who took time out of his day to help me. The gorgeous stranger with hazel eyes full of warmth and shaggy dark brown hair that fell just past his ears. Fit, charming, and far too easy to picture.

I groan and roll to my side trying to get him out of my head. I can't be thinking about how attractive he was. He's about to be my boss, and I'm going to have to work with him every day. Then again, his boss thinks we're together... no! Stop it. I'm barely surviving right now. I can't be thinking about getting involved with anyone. Not that he would want to be involved with me, anyway.

I roll myself over one more time and force myself to fall asleep, hoping Jake stays out of my dreams tonight.

Jake and I arrive at work at the exact same time. I'm about to head inside when he yells my name, which, if I'm being honest, sounds really good coming from him.

"You ready for today?" he asks, avoiding eye contact with me.

What's that about?

"Uh, yeah. I hope I don't suck."

He laughs. "I'm sure you'll be great."

We walk in side by side, yet he still seems to be avoiding my gaze. I glance down to ensure that I have pants and a shirt on, which I do, then make sure I don't have a random hole in my uniform. I don't see anything out of the ordinary. Maybe he's just shy today since it's his first day?

We walk up to the front desk together, and an older lady is waiting for us. She has short gray hair and lots of wrinkles. She must be in her seventies.

"Jake and Jules?" she asks, looking between us.

"Yes," both Jake and I respond at the same time.

She frowns. "Follow me."

Well, she looks like a joy to work for. While her attitude and voice were annoying, my heart couldn't help but react to the way our names sounded together. Jake and Jules.

Shaking my head, I chuckle to myself. What is wrong with me? Stop thinking about this. I'm here to work, make money, and avoid getting kicked out of my apartment.

"What's funny?" Jake asks.

Oops, maybe I didn't chuckle silently like I thought.

"Nothing," I say.

He doesn't push for an answer, and we continue following the old lady through some hallways and staff doors.

We finally make it to a little room that looks like a breakroom. It has a table in the corner, a vending machine, a refrigerator, and a television.

"I'm going to give you all the information you need about housekeeping and our employee handbook. You will read through it all and let me know when you're done. You'll be cleaning rooms together this week, and we aren't going to move on until you do it perfectly," the old lady, who still hasn't told us her name, says.

"Sounds good," Jake replies with a swoon-worthy smile.

How is he so calm and charming all the time? This lady just told us we'd be cleaning rooms all week and to go through like a hundred pages. Isn't he supposed to be the manager?

As if I said my thoughts aloud, the old lady says to Jake, "To be a successful manager, you need to experience what these ladies do. I retire in two weeks, so I hope you're a quick learner."

Ah, she must be the current housekeeping manager, and Jake's taking her position. That makes sense.

"I look forward to learning from you. I do have one question," he states.

"What is it?"

"May I ask your name?" he asks sweetly.

"Joyce," she replies.

"Joyce. What a sophisticated name for a beautiful woman," he says smoothly.

I roll my eyes as I watch her blush. In just these brief interactions with Jake, I can tell he's a ladies' man. It's not just the fact that he's gorgeous and flirty, but he also makes women feel special. Though my heart sinks a little realizing that he hasn't flirted with me. I've already watched him flirt with Tonya and now Joyce. Not that Joyce is any competition.

Joyce and Jake get into their own little conversation as he's clearly won her over. I ignore them and begin reading through the employee manual, which is basic stuff. Don't do anything immoral, don't steal, wear your uniform, etc. By the time I'm on the fifth page, Joyce finally leaves, and Jake brings his attention back to the packet in front of him.

He lifts it, then puts it back down, staring at me. "Anything interesting that I should take note of?"

I look at him and back down at my papers. "You should probably read it yourself."

"Ouch, what did I do to deserve that?" he asks.

I sigh and look back up at him. He's right. He didn't deserve a snarky response like that.

"Sorry, I didn't sleep well last night," I say.

"Want to talk about it?" he asks sincerely.

"Why?"

"Huh?" he looks at me confused.

"Why are you being so nice and helping me when you don't even know me?" I ask, genuinely wanting an answer. The question plagued me all night.

He taps his pen on the desk as if he's thinking over his response before he answers. "Because you looked like you just really needed to catch a break. I've had people helping me lately, so I thought I'd return the favor where I could," he says.

I nod and whisper, "Thank you."

"You're welcome," he says. "Now... do you want to go through this together or continue reading it alone?"

I smile as we go through the handbook together and the checklist of everything that needs to be done inside a hotel room. Jake puts on his charm, and I also get to see his funny side. We joke about half the items and then make up stories about why some rules are stated. Rules are always created out of necessity because someone did it before.

An example is that a housekeeper shouldn't flip the mattress to hide stains... Like, why would you do that? Jake also decided to Google a few things, and sometimes the guests will do that too, which explains why we should be looking under mattresses too. I thought that was a weird rule. According to Google, people do odd rituals or cut open the mattresses... like what? I'm really starting to reconsider staying in hotel rooms.

By the time Joyce comes back to check in on us, we've completed our assigned reading and already feel like good friends. Jake is so easy to be around and talk to. I've been depressed lately, but when he's around, he makes me smile. He makes it feel like everything is going to be okay.

Chapter Four

JAKE

Day one at my new job wasn't as bad as I thought it would be. It was actually a lot of fun. Odd for me to say that considering my current circumstances. I think it would've been much different if Jules hadn't been there with me today. There's just something about her that makes me... feel.

I haven't felt much of anything in... I don't know how long. Months? Years? Regardless, I didn't quite understand what it was at first. When I saw her today in her work uniform, which isn't even remotely sexy, I thought she was the hottest woman on the planet. Maybe I have a thing for housekeepers. Regardless, the moment I saw her, I had to keep myself in check and not look at her. My dick stirred in my pants, which isn't something that has happened since Everly and I broke off our friends-with-benefits arrangement.

Thinking about Everly creates a pang of guilt. She's one of my best friends and has been since we were little kids. We grew closer during our college years, even though we were attending college across the country from each other. She's also the one I was pining after for years, but ultimately, I always knew she'd never be mine.

By now, she knows I'm missing. My brother would've avoided calling her for as long as possible, but after Ben, she'd be the next one to reach out to find me. Since she's on her honeymoon with James, Bash wouldn't have wanted to bother them. The thought of making them worry twists my stomach, but this opportunity my father gave me to disappear for a while is something I can't pass up. There's too much I need to figure out, and dragging them into it would only make things worse. Maybe that's why I'm starting to understand why Everly tried to distance herself from us after she left for college.

I shake my head to chase away thoughts of Everly. Jules slips into my mind instead, and a genuine smile tugs at my lips. Something about that woman sets her apart from anyone I've met before. She's real, and we actually had fun reading through boring paperwork together. Usually, it takes effort to make a situation bearable with my humor, but with her around, I barely had to try.

A car pulling up in front of me catches my attention. I've been waiting on the side of this street for about ten minutes for my friend from college, Rowen Ashford. He's secretive, careful, and a private person. Given the nature of his job, I don't blame him.

I make my way to his car and slide in. He did a drive-by earlier as I was walking back to Eric's apartment, telling me to meet him here at this time. You don't say no to Rowen, so here I am.

"What's up?" I ask as he drives off.

I look over at him and notice he's wearing sunglasses, even though it's dark outside. He has on a beanie that completely covers his blonde hair, and I would bet anything that he's wearing green contact lenses to hide his blue eyes. You know, in case he has to take off his sunglasses.

"We need to talk," he states seriously.

I frown. "Alright, where are we heading?"

"My place."

I don't respond because now I know it's serious. I've only been to his place a few times. I'm pretty sure I'm the only one who's ever been there. The first time I was brought there was when I was at my lowest... I'm not going to think about that right now.

"Is everything okay?" I ask nervously, tapping my fingers against the armrest.

He doesn't respond. Crap. Now my heart is racing, wondering what this could mean. Hopefully everything's okay with him. Hopefully, my family's okay. Why did I cut myself off completely? What if something's happened to my friends or family?

"Everything's fine, Jake," he says to ease my internal panic.

I let out a long breath and nod. We're quiet the rest of the ride to his house, and by his house, I mean his mansion.

We pull up to the front, and his car is scanned before the gate opens. The long driveway leads to the garage, where we park. I follow him to the door leading inside and watch as he unlocks it with his fingerprint. I want to act surprised, but I've seen it all before. He's cautious, always thinking several steps ahead.

Once we get inside, he sets down his hat, sunglasses, and keys. I slip off my shoes and follow him through the sleek, pristine kitchen into the living room. On the surface, it looks like any normal house, but I know better. Beneath us lies a basement filled with rooms of glowing monitors and humming security systems. Beyond that, there is a bunker and a subterranean garden, a place where he could disappear and survive for years without ever stepping outside. Every corner of this house whispers control, precision, and danger.

I sink into a dark brown chair while he takes the one across from me, with the coffee table stretching out between us.

"Want anything to drink?" he asks.

"I'm good," I say, wanting to get this over with.

He stares at me, and I stare back into his green eyes, the contacts I knew he was wearing. Neither of us speaks, but the tension between us is thick. Sweat drips down the back of my neck.With a nervous laugh, I say, "Alright man, you gotta give me something."

He leans back, getting comfortable. "Your brother reached out to me."

I nod. "I figured he would."

Bash knows Rowen, but not as Rowen. He knows him as Hank, who is a hacker and can find out pretty much anything. He's great at what he does and has many clients. No one knows who Hank really is, except me.

"You need to talk to me before I make a decision on what to tell him."

My heart races. I don't know why I'm so nervous about talking to Rowen. He has always been there for me. Like I said, he has seen me at my lowest. Not even my family has seen the side of me that he has and still does.

"I don't want to be found," I state, hoping he won't ask me any further questions, but I know better.

"You have to give me more than that. I'm already struggling with something he brought to me months ago, so if I'm going to fail him again, I need a good reason," he states casually.

I sigh. "I just need time. My father disowned me, and I need some time to think."

"Can't you just go on a vacation to think? You have to disappear?"

I shake my head. "Come on, man. I have nothing to my name anymore."

"Where are you staying?" he asks seriously.

"Eric's apartment."

He cocks his eyebrow. "Everly's Eric?"

I groan as I continue telling him the story of how everything went down that night at the bar with Eric. Then how I got a job at Tristan's hotel and how I met Jules. I'd say it probably sounds crazy to him, but he's seen crazier.

"Alright, I'll keep him off your trail for as long as I can."

"Thank you, Rowen. I owe you," I say sincerely.

He shakes his head. "You know you'll never owe me anything."

I do. He's the most selfless friend you'll ever find. He can be a jerk at times, but it's all because he loves you. He's saved me more times than I can count. Our friendship started back in college when we had a couple of classes together. I noticed his high school bullies followed him to college, and I had his back, taking care of the situation. Ever since then, he's had mine and taken care of me.

I'm not getting into thinking about that right now. "So how is it coming with Bash's issue?"

My brother called Hank a while ago because there was a security breach at his company and at his buddy's company. They've been having a tough time finding out who it is that keeps hacking their systems, but I know that Rowen will be able to find them.

"I'm close. I've found out that it's a girl, which has me intrigued. She's good, almost my level good."

I cock an eyebrow at him. "How do you know it's a girl?"

He rolls his eyes. "She's cocky, and she wanted me to know. She's been leaving me messages."

I laugh. "Wow. Is this some weird flirting thing she's doing with you?"

He groans. "She's getting on my nerves. She's going to mess up eventually though, and I'm going to be there the day she does."

"I know you will. Well, I'm invested, so keep me updated," I say.

"Speaking of..." he says before getting up and heading to the other room.

I watch him leave the room and reenter less than a minute later with a phone. He hands it to me.

"What's it for?" I ask.

"It's a phone, idiot. You didn't have one, but now you do."

"I don't want it."

"Too bad. If you want me to keep your family and friends off your trail, then you better keep it with you. Everyone's numbers are programmed in there, but it's a new number, so no one has it."

"Alright, thanks," I say, pocketing it. I don't want to know how he got my contact list and uploaded it to this phone.

"And here." He hands me a card. "It's a new bank account that can't be traced. I assume you asked Tristan to pay you under the table?"

I take it and nod. I did ask Tristan not to put my information through the system because I know that anyone with half the skills of Rowen would be able to find me that way. He's paying me in cash.

"Just be careful, and I'd wear hats and sunglasses in public. He might get tired of waiting for me and hire someone else.

They could easily find you with cameras around the city. I also put in some money to get you started," he says.

I interrupt him. "I don't want your money."

He shakes his head. "It isn't mine. It's your brother's. I'm giving you what he paid me to find you. Since I'm not actually going to do that, I don't feel right keeping it."

I groan. I don't want to take any handouts, but I also get what he's saying. When I get back on my feet, I'll pay him back.

As if he's reading my mind, he puts up a hand saying, "If you really want to pay it back, then return it to your brother as a refund from Hank."

I laugh. "Alright, fine. I appreciate everything, as always."

"You sure you're good to stay at Eric's?" he asks.

"Yeah, I'm good there." I stand, hoping he's going to let this be the end of it.

"Alright, I'll bring you home, but just one more question, and I need a serious answer." He stands in front of me, looking me dead in the eye, placing his hands on my shoulders. "You're okay?"

I nod. "Yeah, I'm okay."

That question has a deeper meaning to it, one that I promised I would never lie to him about, and I won't. He's the only one I can be completely honest with. One that holds no judgement, and one that has my back unconditionally.

He pats me on the back. "Good, but you'll tell me immediately if that changes. Let's go."

It's not a question. It's a demand. I push down any emotions he's bringing out of me and walk behind him to his car so he can take me back to Eric's place.

CHAPTER FIVE
JULES

Today is the last workday of my first week. I've been burying myself in tasks, clinging to the routine, trying not to think about my reality. But it's impossible to escape. My life has crumbled. Everything I poured myself into, everything I worked so hard for, has slipped through my fingers and washed down the drain.

Ugh, this isn't the time to think about this. I'm walking to work in the pouring rain. Thankfully, I have a nice raincoat, rain boots, and umbrella, but it's still depressing. What's also depressing is that today will be the last day that Jake and I work closely together.

We've been cleaning rooms together, just the two of us, all week. He's the funniest, most charming man I have ever worked with. Somehow, he stays positive and takes everything in stride. He has yet to complain about a single thing. Vomit on the bed? Whatever, they must have had a fun night. Blood all over the floor in the bathroom? Let's come up with a crazy murder story here.

I don't know much of anything about Jake, but I want to get to know him. When I'm around him, it's like nothing bad can happen, or at least, he'll make it better. I decided I'm going to get the courage to ask him for his phone number today. Mainly under the pretense of our boss thinking we're in love, which we still haven't discussed.

I jump as thunder startles me out of my thoughts. I'm only a block away from work… I can do this. Just as I think that, water splashes all over me from a car passing by. I freeze, standing still, wondering if that just really happened. My raincoat and boots took the brunt of it, but I still have my knees down exposed and now wet… and cold. Very cold. I growl as I walk faster to get to the hotel.

I step into the building, close my umbrella, and start peeling off my raincoat. Before I even hear his voice, I feel him. Jake. My body goes rigid as he steps up behind me and takes the coat from my hands.

I cringe as I push my drenched hair back. "Ugh, don't look at me. I'm a drowned rat."

He stands in front of me smirking, pushing my hair back. "A beautiful drowned rat."

My heart skips a beat as I process what he just said. Did he just call me beautiful? He's yet to say anything like that to me, nor flirt with me. I've seen him casually flirting with pretty much every single woman in this building that he has come across, except me.

"Thanks," I say, not knowing how else to reply.

"There are extra clothes in the back if you want to change," he says, and I follow him.

I didn't know that. I guess it makes sense. They had a uniform for me to take home immediately after I got hired. I quickly change my pants in the bathroom and head back to where Jake is waiting for me. Since it's the last day working closely with him, I figure it's the only opportunity I'm going to have to get him alone to discuss the whole our boss thinks we're together thing.

"Hey, can we talk really quick?" I ask nervously.

"Sure," he says while putting down his clipboard.

I grab his arm and tug him toward one of the supply closets. Not wanting anyone overhearing us, I shove him inside and click the door shut behind us. I haven't turned on the light yet, and my hands fumble over the switch until it flicks on. Then I realize I'm chest to chest with Jake. Heat rises in my cheeks, and my stomach flips. I can feel the warmth radiating from him, and suddenly the closet feels impossibly small.

I gasp and back up. "Sorry!"

He laughs and places his hand on my hip to steady me. "If you wanted to have some fun, you could've just asked."

"No, I..." I clear my throat and shake my head. "Sorry, I didn't want anyone to hear our conversation."

He cocks an eyebrow at me. Ugh, why is that so sexy? Okay, stop. This man would never go for someone like me.

"So, as you know, our boss thinks we're together. We haven't talked about what that means yet or looks like," I say.

He thinks for a moment before responding. "What do you think that looks like?"

I shrug. "I don't know. I really need to keep this job, and I just want to make sure that he doesn't find out we lied."

"We didn't really lie. We just let him think what he wanted without correcting him," he says, shrugging his shoulders.

"Yeah, I guess... but it's still a lie. Should we like, do lunch or something together some days? I figure we won't be seeing each other much at work after today, so being intentional about seeing each other at lunch would prove we're together," I ramble.

He smirks. God, he's so hot. "Are you asking me out on a date, Jules?"

I facepalm myself and groan. "No... I..."

He stops me by placing a hand on my shoulder. "I'd love to have lunch with you every day."

Every day? I just said that we'd have lunch some days, though every day would work. We work the same schedule because Tristan thought we might commute together since we're a couple. Well, fake couple, obviously.

"Okay," I whisper.

"Also, I think I should probably have your phone number. You know, since you're my fake girlfriend."

"Right. Um yeah, that makes sense," I say, stumbling over my words and then rattling off my number as he enters it into his phone.

My phone vibrates shortly after as he says, "Just sent you mine."

I nod and wait for him to either say something else or make the first move out of the closet. This ridiculously hot closet. When did it get so hot in here?

Suddenly, he leans forward with his face inches from mine. My breath catches as I watch him continue to lean in closer and closer. Is he about to... kiss me? I'm taken from my thoughts when the door opens behind me, and I realize he was leaning to grab the door handle. Duh. What is wrong with me?

"Alright, thanks. See you in a few minutes," I say as I duck under his arm and race out of the closet feeling embarrassed.

A few minutes later, after cooling off in the bathroom, I find Jake standing outside the first hotel room we're scheduled to clean with a grimace on his face.

"What's wrong?" I ask.

"I think they decided to save the hardest for last," he says, opening the door.

I peek past him, and my stomach sinks. The room is a complete disaster. We've seen some pretty gross places before, but this one takes it to another level. Bedding is strewn across the floor, and trash covers every surface. Beer cans, takeout boxes, and scraps of food litter the tables and floor, mingling with the sheets. A wet, sticky streak runs down the wall, making my skin crawl. I hesitate to step further inside, especially toward the bathroom.

"I can't imagine leaving a hotel room like this," I say, cringing.

"These are expensive rooms, so they are probably rich kids who think the world owes them everything," Jake states with disgust.

"Well, they will have to pay for the state they left it in," I say.

"I doubt they'll even blink at the charge," he says while putting his gloves on and getting to work.

"Wow," I say.

"What?" He stops what he's doing and stares at me.

"I've never heard you like this before."

"Like what?" he asks.

"I don't know... upset? Usually you're so positive, and nothing brings you down. You must really have a thing against wealthy people," I observe.

He laughs and shakes his head. "You're right, sorry. I just had a moment."

"Don't apologize. It's okay to have moments and not always be happy. Honestly, it was nice seeing. I don't know much about you."

He looks me over for a moment before responding. "You're right. I don't know much about you either, other than I enjoy spending time with you. We'll have to remedy that over our lunch dates."

My stomach does somersaults hearing the word lunch dates come out of his mouth. Does he really mean that? Does he want to get to know me better? Does he consider them actual dates? As much as I feel like I'm drowning in my own life, it sounds kind of nice to have someone to share my time with. I don't have any friends. When I moved to New York, it was for one reason and one reason only. To be successful on Broadway.

The "friends" I made here were never real friends. We were all clawing for the bigger and better roles, and most of the women were catty and jealous. I never truly clicked with anyone, and honestly, I didn't try to. It's been lonely. Since I started ignoring my brother, it's been even lonelier.

As I scrub the bathroom, a small smile tugs at my lips. Maybe, just maybe, I could finally have someone to confide in. Maybe I could even have something a little more than friendship with Jake.

CHAPTER SIX

JAKE

It's seven at night, and I've already had three beers. I have tomorrow off, but wish I didn't. Staying busy at work has been a lifeline, keeping my mind from spiraling. The exhaustion from a day spent running ragged ensures I sleep, even if only temporarily, without getting lost in my own thoughts.

I stare at Eric's television screen, feeling every ounce of motivation drain out of me. I groan and take another sip of beer, trying to push away the weight of my current life. My head shakes almost involuntarily as I stand and make my way to the bathroom, wishing the world would just let me catch a break.

I stare at myself in the mirror as the water runs over my hands. The face staring back looks like a stranger. If I'm honest, I'm not sure I've ever truly recognized the person looking back at me. What have I done with my life?

My gaze drifts to the pill bottle peeking out of my bag on the counter. Oxycodone. The prescription from last year when I fractured a rib sparring with Bash. My eyes linger on the label far longer than they should. For a heartbeat, I picture twisting the cap, downing a few, letting the world blur and quiet for a while. The thought is dangerous, but in this moment it's tempting.

My phone buzzes with a text, taking my attention away from the bottle. I debate looking at it but then remember only four people have this number. Eric, Rowen, Tristan, and Jules. I sigh as I see it's a text from Rowen.

Rowen

Still running clean?

I stare at his message, debating how to respond. How does he always know when I start getting in my head? Does he have some sort of device that he can hear my thoughts? Knowing him, I wouldn't be surprised if he does. Just to see if so, I say to myself silently, "Dude, if you can hear me, text me again."

No such text comes through. I shrug my shoulders. He probably wouldn't tell me if he did have a device in my head, anyway. Ugh, what is wrong with me? That's insane.

Holding steady.

That's not exactly a lie. My thoughts had wandered dangerously close, but I didn't go through with it. Would I have if Rowen hadn't interrupted them? I shake my head, leave the bathroom, and flop back onto the couch. I finish my beer, then toss the empty can across the room into the recycling bin. Made it!

Rowen responds.

Rowen

Let me know if that changes.

I drag my hand through my hair. Rowen's a good friend, but sometimes I wish he wasn't. These texts are his way of checking to make sure my mental health is okay. He personally diagnosed me with depression, even though I've never seen a doctor or therapist about it. I tried to deny it for a while, but there's been a few times in my life where I've gotten so far into my head that I didn't even care if I lived or died.

Sometimes it's for good reason, while other times it just hits out of nowhere. I get to where I can't eat or even get out of bed. At those times, I've always claimed that I was taking a vacation and doing what everyone thought I always did... had lots of booze and women. I didn't correct them because I thought that was a better alternative than my father knowing that I was depressed. Mental health issues don't exist in his mind, and I'd be considered weak or lazy. He already thinks poorly of me, so I didn't want to give him more ammunition.

My brother and friends don't know either. To them, I'm always happy and carefree. Why? Because they have enough shit going on in their lives and don't need to worry about me. I know how much it sucks to be depressed, so I want to do everything in my power to make sure everyone around me is happy.

What makes it worse is the guilt. Every time I sink into that dark place, a voice in my head starts shouting at me. What right do I have to feel this way? My family and friends are billionaires. I have more money than I could ever spend, can have almost any woman I want, and don't have any major health issues. I'm one of the luckiest men alive. And yet, I still feel like I'm drowning. The guilt of feeling this way only drags me deeper.

I thought I had it under control until Rowen found me almost dead a few years ago. I wasn't paying attention, or I just didn't care about how much drugs and alcohol I had consumed. Accidentally cutting my wrist that day put an idea in my head... I took it too far. I'm not suicidal by any means, but I don't think I would've cared in that moment if I had died, which led to me feeling even more guilty. Everly lost one of her best friends to suicide, which affected us all, especially her since she found her the next morning. So, I made a promise to Rowen to let him know when I got to that point, and he made a promise that if he ever found me like that again he'd force me to get help and would tell my family.

Either way, I feel myself slipping, and that's not good. I need to find something to occupy my mind while I'm off work for the next two days. Especially right now.

As if the universe is throwing me a bone, Eric walks into the apartment.

"Hey, how was your week?" he asks as he lays his stuff down on the counter.

I raise my new beer to him. "Good. How about you?"

"Busy. I don't feel like I've been home all week," he says.

I laugh. "You weren't kidding about that. Explains the lack of décor too."

He looks around as if he hadn't noticed. "Yeah, it is pretty depressing, isn't it? I don't know... I don't feel like it's home."

Well, yeah, it's hard to feel like this is home when it looks like no one lives here. I'm not going to say anything though because I kind of get it.

He grabs himself a beer and sits on the couch next to me. "Any plans tomorrow?"

"Nope. I figure I'll spend some time going over finances and looking for apartments, but other than that I've got nothing," I say a little too cheerfully.

He takes a swig of his beer. "Me neither. Stay here for as long as you want and save some money. As you can see, I'm rarely home."

"I appreciate it," I say.

"Want to hit the gym with me in the morning?" he asks.

I forgot his apartment complex has a gym. I've been so exhausted I haven't even thought about working out, which is usually crucial to keeping my head demons at bay.

"Yeah, what time?" I ask.

"I usually hit it around 6:30."

I nod, more to myself than anyone else. Spending time with Eric is probably the smartest thing I can do right now. At least it'll keep me from slipping too far into my own head. I don't have my brother anymore. Or Ben. Just thinking their names feels like someone pressing a thumb into a fresh wound. The next two days are going to be hell, and I know it. I've been moving so fast I haven't let myself process any of it. If I don't find a way to stop and deal with it soon, it's all going to pile up until it explodes. I'm terrified of what that's going to look like when it does.

Nope, I didn't give myself any time to process the mess my life has become. Eric was off the same two days I was, so we spent the entire time together. If someone had told me years ago that I'd actually want to hang out with him and enjoy it, I would've laughed in their face.

Eric is a really cool guy. I kind of knew that when I hung out with him and Everly, but I never had guy time with him. Working in the financial field, I always thought he was boring. We decided to shake things up a bit. He claims he hasn't made many friends around here and misses doing the little things.

We spent the nights at bars drinking and flirting with women, but during the days we acted like high schoolers. We went to an arcade, bowling, a movie theater, and played miniature golf. I didn't realize how competitive he was until now.

Of course he paid for everything, even though I insisted I had money. Which is true, because Rowen gave me a lot, but I can't tell him that. I've been keeping track so I can be sure to pay him back. When that's going to be, I have no idea. I don't need to figure that out right this second though because I have to finish getting ready for work.

After I make myself some coffee, Eric comes out fully dressed for work. He makes one for himself and then stares at his phone.

"Still nothing?" I ask.

He shakes his head and sighs. "She said maybe she'll come over next weekend."

"That's good! Isn't it?"

"Nah, when she says maybe, it never happens. I don't know what to do," he says, looking lost.

I think for a second. "Then don't ask her to hang out. Ask her for help. Think of something she won't say no to."

His face lights up. "Why didn't I think of that?! She can't say no to helping others. Thanks, man."

Eric types out a message and sends it to his sister. I hope it works, because this is something he talked about a lot this weekend. I never got her name, only ever hearing him call her "my sis." They used to see each other every week, but for the past couple of months she's been avoiding him. He can tell something's wrong, even if she keeps denying it. Seeing her in person will tell him more than any text ever could.

I try not to think too much about Bash while he talks about her. I can only imagine he's going crazy not knowing where I am. I'm sure my father spun some story about me being on vacation, partying with no cell service.

That familiar dread creeps through me, but I shove it aside. Nope. Too early to let my thoughts go there. I need to focus on work, and for once, I'm actually looking forward to it. After all, I get to have lunch with Jules today.

Things are tense the moment I get to work. Jules is on her own cleaning rooms, and Joyce decided she didn't want to work anymore, so I'm left to my own devices as manager after only one week of training. Shortly before lunch, Tristan calls me into his office. Great.

His door is open when I get there, so I knock on the doorframe before entering.

He looks up from his desk. "Hey! Come in!"

I smile wide and give him a bro hug with a pat to the back when he stands. "How's it going?"

He grins. "I should be asking you that. Sorry Joyce ditched early, but I'm sure you've got it covered."

I nod. "Of course."

"Still enjoying the job?" he asks, sitting back down behind his desk.

I follow suit and sit in the chair across from him. "It's great. You have no idea how much I appreciate you doing this for me."

"Anything for you, Jake, but I was hoping you'd be begging to help me up here after day one," he laughs.

I laugh too. "Nah, this is perfect."

He turns serious. "How do you always do that?"

"What?" I ask, confused.

"How are you always so positive? Your entire life was turned upside down, and yet you're thankful for getting a housekeeping job at my hotel when you're used to being at the top."

That feeling of dread spreads through me again, heavy and cold. Why did he have to bring that up? How am I supposed to answer that? He doesn't really want the truth. He doesn't want to hear that staying positive is the only thing keeping me from drowning myself in drugs and alcohol. He doesn't want to know that without it, I'd probably be lying in bed all day, or worse, on the street, not caring what happened to me. No, he doesn't want that answer, and I can't give it to him.

I shrug my shoulders, trying hard to keep a smile on my face. "I'm still breathing, so what's there not to be positive about?"

When in doubt, just divert by asking a question back. He shakes his head and chuckles.

"Well, I've had nothing but compliments coming from the housekeeping department about you," he says.

"Really?" I ask in shock.

"Seems the ladies love you, as always."

I laugh again. "Ah, yes."

"You still with Jules?" he asks, and it looks like there's a hint of hope in his eyes that I'm not.

"I am. We're actually about to head to lunch together," I say.

"Well, that's great. No one has mentioned anything between you two, so it seems you're doing a good job keeping it professional," he says.

"Yep. We act like we barely know each other." Which is the truth.

"Well I hope you have a good lunch. Let me know if I can help with anything."

I shake his hand before leaving. "Thanks, boss."

Now, I can finally see the one person I've been looking forward to seeing all day.

Chapter Seven

Jules

Finally. I'm finally having lunch with Jake, which I have been looking forward to for days. I debated texting him while we were off, but I didn't want to seem too clingy. I mean, we had just spent the entire week together working side by side. He deserved a couple of days away from me.

I'm not going to lie though, I checked my phone a few too many times in hopes that I had missed a text from him. Each time I looked at my phone, a pang of disappointment hit. I don't know why. It's not like Jake and I are actually dating. Heck, I don't even know his last name or favorite color. I'll have to remedy that quickly.

"What's your favorite color?" I blurt out as he's looking over the menu.

He places the menu down and smiles. "Black."

I stare at him. "Black is not a color. It's a shade."

He leans back casually, with his arm resting on the back of the chair. "That's what people say when they don't want to admit it looks good with everything."

I smile. "So that's it? You like it because it's flattering?"

He shrugs and picks his menu back up. "I like that it doesn't draw attention. It's quiet."

That surprises me. He doesn't seem like the kind of man who wants to disappear and hide in the shadows. He's so charismatic and seems like the center of attention whenever he walks into a room.

"You like quiet?" I ask.

"I do now," he says, not looking up from his menu.

There's something in his voice that doesn't allow me to respond to that. Something tired. I really don't know anything about his past or how he got here. For some reason, I want to know everything about this man.

"My favorite is turquoise," I say, taking the conversation off him.

"Is there a reason why?" he asks curiously, with his attention on me again.

I shrug. "Yeah, it reminds me of the beach, of a time that was fun when I was a kid. When everything was lighter. A time that I thought I could do anything..."

He says nothing in response. He watches me quietly, waiting for me to continue. Do I want to continue? I mean, why not? He's my fake boyfriend, and honestly, I don't have anyone else to talk to. If I want to get to know about his life, I have to be willing to share mine.

Just as I'm about to continue, the waitress comes over to take our orders. We both order the same burgers, and again, I'm surprised. He seems like he would have a strict, healthy diet and work out every day with how fit he looks.

Once she leaves, I decide to go ahead and get it out in the open. "I worked my butt off my whole life learning how to sing and dance. I always dreamed of being on Broadway, so I moved to New York knowing I'd land a role, and I did."

He's looking at me intently, like he's really interested in learning about my life. It gives me the courage to continue.

"My very first day, I landed wrong on my leg, and it forever ruined my career as a dancer," I say, shrugging my shoulders, trying to downplay how much it affects me.

"When did that happen?" he asks.

"A couple of months ago," I reply again like it's just a random story to tell.

"That's super shitty. I can't even imagine having a dream for your whole life, to be given it, and then having it ripped away like that," he reaches out and covers my hand with his. "I'm sorry."

I look away because it's the only thing I can do to keep the tears from spilling. Wow. I've cried over this so much. It's not necessarily just the situation, but it's him. He's making me so emotional with the way he sincerely cares and understands what I'm saying. I figured most people would just say I'm sorry, but you have to move on or something to that effect. "Do you have family around?" he asks.

Ugh, now guilt is starting to surface. "Yeah, my brother lives here. My parents are back in Georgia."

He tilts his head and asks, "Are you and your brother close?"

I fidget with my hair. "We are, or were. I haven't really talked to him much since it happened. In fact, I haven't told him yet."

"Why?"

I shrug. "I don't know. I guess I wanted to figure things out first before telling him."

He leans back in his chair again and sighs. "Yeah, I understand that completely."

I straighten in my chair. "Alright, now tell me about yourself. I just told you my darkest secrets. Your turn."

I try to say it lightly, jokingly even, but he looks at me like he carries demons of his own. His fingers drum against the table, and he doesn't answer. A creeping unease settles in my chest. Is he going to shut down completely? I'm starting to regret asking.

I clear my throat. "I was just kidding. You don't have to tell me anything you don't want to."

He gives a small smile. "Nah, why not? I'm in a similar situation where I'm trying to figure out where to go with my life. My father disowned me, and I left with just a few twenties in my wallet and a duffle of essentials. I'm relying on an old acquaintance by staying in his guest room and using Tristan to get this job. I have no idea where my life is going to go from here."

Wow. "I never would've guessed. You look so put together all the time and… happy."

He laughs and runs his hand through his hair. Looks like we both have the same nervous tick. "Appearances can be deceiving."

I nod. Yeah, they can. I hate that he's going through all that, but in a way, I'm glad he is. I'm glad to have someone to commiserate with. We're both stuck at crappy jobs so we can pay the bills and have no idea where we're going with our lives.

"Do you have any siblings?" I ask.

"Yeah, my brother lives here," he says.

"Why aren't you living with him?"

He slouches back in his chair. "I guess for the same reason you haven't spoken to your brother. I want to figure out my life before going to him. He likes to fix things, and I don't need that right now."

"Wow, we're really living the same life, aren't we?" I laugh. "My brother is the same way. If he found out, he'd go into fix-it mode."

Our burgers arrive, and I pig out. Usually when on a date, I don't eat much. I feel too nervous to eat, but with Jake, I don't feel that at all. Maybe it's because this isn't a real date, but I have a feeling that's not what it is. Jake's just really easy to talk to.

We move onto lighter conversation that doesn't involve our pasts and discuss just our interests. Favorite TV shows, movies, animals, sports, etc. The easy stuff. The stuff friends talk about. Lunch goes by quickly, and I'm sad when we head back to work.

"Do you want to hang out tonight?" he asks.

Butterflies form in my stomach. Did he just ask me out on a real date? I think for a moment before replying. Do I want to go on a real date with Jake? I don't have my life together yet. Would it be smart to have a boyfriend? Stop overthinking. He's not asking me to be his girlfriend. He's just asking to hang out.

"As friends," he adds, noticing I'm taking too long to respond.

My heart sinks. Oh. Yeah. Friends, of course. "Sure. What do you have in mind?"

He gives a devious grin. "It's a surprise."

I chuckle. "I love surprises."

"Really?" he asks.

"Yeah, why?"

He shrugs. "Not many people like surprises."

"What about you? Do you like surprises?" I ask.

He thinks about it for a moment. "I guess it depends on the surprise."

I laugh. "That's a no, then."

"Is it?" He smirks, his hand sliding to the small of my back as he guides me toward the door.

Those little butterflies start fluttering again at his touch. I try to force them to calm down. He made it clear we're just friends, but they won't listen. It's been a while since I've had a boyfriend. No, it's been forever. I laugh quietly to myself. I tried dating for a few weeks in high school, but the guy gave up on me because I was too busy. After that, I decided to focus on my career. Once I got to where I wanted to be, I could think about dating again.

Yeah, this is for the best. I don't really have friends, so having Jake as a friend is perfect. I definitely don't have my life together, so I shouldn't be thinking about a relationship.

Once we make it back to work, we go our separate ways, and I miss him already. He said we'll head out together after work, and that's enough to get me through the rest of my shift.

CHAPTER EIGHT

JAKE

I have no fucking idea what I'm doing. The last thing I should be doing is asking Jules out on a date. I'm glad she hesitated because it put into perspective that we need to just remain friends. I'm literally running away from my life right now. There's no way I can add in the complication of a woman.

A really amazing woman. One that is just like me. I knew there was some darkness swimming around in that head of hers. It's like my darkness seeks others. I've been down this road before with some old buddies, and it didn't end well. We encouraged each other to feel better with drugs and alcohol. Those relationships were toxic, and I'm hoping this one doesn't turn into that.

My problem is that I can't seem to get her out of my mind. Ever since Everly broke off our friends-with-benefits arrangement, I haven't felt remotely anything for another woman. Emotional or physical. Jules makes me feel both, which is a problem in itself. The only action I've gotten since Everly is with my own hand. Yeah, that means it has been a ridiculous number of years since I've gotten laid. Since I've wanted to get laid.

I even questioned myself once, thinking maybe I just didn't like women anymore. But that's not it. I've had more than enough chances over the years, but I just never wanted any of them. Women basically throw themselves at me, and I know why. Yeah, I know I'm good-looking, but it's all about the money. It's always about money. Jules doesn't seem to care about that though, which is another positive for me.

I met Jules in the lobby after work, grateful I didn't have to put much thought into this non-date. I had already planned on doing it one day this week anyway. It always clears my head, and I needed that. After hearing everything she shared over lunch, I figured she could use it too. Besides, it's better with a friend.

"Ready?" I ask, but she looks nervous.

"Um... well..." she starts, but doesn't continue.

"What is it?" I ask, hoping she isn't about to back out.

She shakes her head. "I didn't bring any clothes to change into, and I don't really want to go out with these on."

She gestures to what she's wearing, and I personally don't see a problem. Okay, my dick doesn't see a problem, but I understand. They aren't the most flattering clothes, and she's been wearing them all day cleaning up people's bodily fluids and who knows what else.

"Do you want to go back to your place to change first?" I ask.

She nods. "If you don't mind."

"How far is it?"

"It's about thirty minutes from here with the subway and walking," she says.

"Alright, let's go." I place my hand on her lower back.

This is the second time today I've put my hand on her lower back like she belongs to me. I honestly didn't mean to do it either time, but it's like I just can't be around her without touching her.

When we reach her apartment building, she acts nervous, like she's not sure what to do. I bet she's freaking out wondering whether or not she should invite me up. She probably thinks it would be rude to keep me waiting outside in the cold, but then she doesn't want to give the wrong idea of the reason she'd be inviting me up. I decide to throw her a bone.

"I can wait out here for you," I say as we walk up the steps.

She shivers from the cold. "No, it's too cold to make you do that. Come up."

"Okay," I state. Now I'm nervous.

Once we enter the building, we walk up a few flights of stairs. Before she unlocks her door, she turns around to look at me.

"So... I wasn't expecting anyone over today... or ever. My place is kind of a mess." Her laugh is nervous, like she's both joking and mortified.

"It's fine. I'm not here to judge the amount of filth you live in," I tease.

She laughs. "Alright, I'll hold you to that."

After unlocking the door, I follow her inside. I take a quick look around and am shocked that it is actually messy. Normally when women would invite me over and claim it was a mess, it was pristine with maybe a book or some papers out of place.

A loveseat is buried under a pile of clothes, with a hamper sitting beside the coffee table. The table itself is cluttered with papers, books, a coffee mug, and other odds and ends. To the left, a small kitchen with a countertop island is just as crowded, every surface covered. At least the floor is clear, though a scatter of shoes lines the wall by the entryway. Something tells me if I opened the entry closet, it would be overflowing.

She cringes as she looks around. "Yeah, it's pretty bad. I'm sorry."

I smirk. "You're right. I take it back. I'm totally judging."

"Really?" Her little smile deflates.

I laugh. "No! I'm joking. I lived in a frat house in college. I've seen a lot of things. This doesn't even come close."

She stares at me for a moment. "I can totally see you living in a frat house."

"What's that supposed to mean?" I ask.

She shrugs her shoulders. "Nothing... You just... look like it."

I gasp and place my hand over my heart playfully. "Are you judging me now?"

She laughs this time. "Not at all. Alright, I'm going to get changed. Any suggestions on what I should wear?"

Oh, I have plenty of suggestions of what I would want to see her wearing, but I'm not here for that. "I'd say something warm for the outside and comfortable for walking and climbing."

"Climbing?" she asks.

"No questions!"

"Alright, alright. I'll be back in a minute," she giggles as she walks off.

I watch her throw a few items that are on the couch in the laundry basket, like she's trying to tidy up on the way to her bedroom. Once she closes herself in her room, I make my way over to the couch and start snooping around. Looking into the laundry basket, I see a black bra and panties on top. She must have been embarrassed that those were lying out and didn't want me to see them.

Even though they're perfectly normal and not even meant to be sexy, just imagining her in them sets something off inside me. I step away, pressing my back against the wall, arms crossed tight. It's maddening. No woman has sparked this in me for years, and now, of all times, she appears and does exactly that. The timing couldn't be more impossible, more infuriating.

She emerges from her room a couple of minutes later in black leggings and an oversized black hoodie, with her hair done in a braid and glasses on. She must wear contacts while working. I've never really been attracted to the nerdy type of girls with glasses, but damn she makes it work.

"What?" she asks as I'm staring at her.

I step in front of her to get a closer look. "I really like you with glasses."

She averts her gaze, and her cheeks turn red. Dammit. Why does she have to be so cute?

"Thanks," she says quietly, like she's not sure how to respond.

I clear my throat. "Alright, let's go."

"You can't be serious," she says, grabbing my arm to pull me back.

I smirk. "I am."

She looks around as if there are police watching and just waiting for us to take a step forward.

"And you've done this before?" she asks uncertainly.

"Yes, many times. I promise it'll be fine."

She looks around again and then lets out a deep breath. "Okay. Let's do it."

I hand her the takeout bag of greasy pizza and sodas, then jump up and latch onto the fire escape ladder. It drops with a heavy thud before clicking into place. She freezes, holding her breath as her eyes dart around, checking if anyone heard. I love that she's so nervous.

I climb the ladder first and step onto the fire escape, keeping an eye on her as she follows. I offer a hand whenever I can, making the climb easier. We don't speak, silence stretching as we ascend, until finally we reach the rooftop. After helping her up, I set the food on the ledge and watch her take in the view.

"Wow," she says breathlessly.

"I told you it would be worth it," I say with a smile, watching her and not paying attention to the view.

"How did you find this?" she asks, finally looking over at me.

As we get settled on the roof, I reply, "My buddy lived here a few years ago. I still come here when I need to clear my head."

She takes a bite of pizza and lets out a soft moan that's far too adorable for my sanity. Heat shoots through me instantly, and I have to tear my eyes away from her. The last thing I need right now is to dwell on the way that sound is doing things to me I shouldn't be thinking about.

"This is the best pizza I've ever had," she says.

I laugh. "Really? It's the cheapest pizza around and probably made in a dirty old kitchen."

She continues to devour it. "I don't care. It's so good, and the view is amazing." She pauses to glance at me, a teasing spark in her eyes. "And I guess the company is good too."

"Oh, just good?" I grin, bumping her shoulder with mine.

She smirks around another bite. "Don't get a big head. The pizza's still winning."

I clutch my chest in mock offense. "Ouch. Reduced to second place behind pizza."

"Second?" she says, licking a bit of sauce off her thumb. "More like third. The view's definitely ahead of you too."

I can't help but grin, her laughter and teasing echoing in my chest. We finish eating in comfortable silence, staring off at the view with the city lights flickering around us. I'm curious what she's thinking about. I don't have the nerve to ask. We've only started getting to know each other today, but we've had some deep conversations. I feel like I need to do what I do best... make everything better.

I pull out my phone and hit shuffle on my music playlist. Of course, the song that pops up is one of the dumb ones I haven't deleted out of spite to annoy my brother.

Jules tilts her head. "This is the type of music you listen to?"

I shrug my shoulders.

She smiles. "So you're more of a pop-punk heartbreak than sad indie boy?"

"Layers, Jules. Like an onion."

She laughs, hard. "I found your new nickname."

"What's that?" I ask curiously.

"Onion, of course."

I shake my head. We continue listening to the music for a moment as it plays softly under the city sounds. Horns blaring, wind blowing, and someone yelling two blocks away.

After coming back from embarrassing myself with the poor song choice, I get the courage to do what I had planned. I stand and dance like an idiot to the music as she watches in disbelief.

"What are you doing?" She's trying to hold back a laugh.

"Dancing?"

She shakes her head and stands up. "That is not dancing."

"Oh yeah? Like you can do any better." It's a dare.

"I'm a dancer..." she pauses for a moment. "Was a dancer. Alright, you're an embarrassment. Let me show you how to dance."

She doesn't give me time to object before she's grabbing one of my hands to put on her waist and holds the other.

"Alright, take a step with your left foot first. One... two... three..."

Trying to follow her lead, my foot lands squarely on hers on the third beat. It looks like I'm either drunk or have never done this before, which isn't exactly true. A pang of guilt hits as I hope I didn't hurt her.

"Ow," she says jokingly. "You're terrible."

I laugh. "Sorry. You saw my dance moves before pulling me into this."

She shakes her head. "Alright, let's keep trying. Just try to stick to the beat and watch your feet."

I do what she said and concentrate on not stepping on her again. We dance through the song without another word or faltering.

"Alright, you're not hopeless," she jokes.

Another song comes on, and it's a fast, upbeat one. She pulls away and starts dancing.

"Try to copy me," she says, spinning around with effortless grace.

I follow her lead, trying to keep up, though I keep pausing, distracted by the way she moves. She looks so carefree, the happiest I've ever seen her. It sucks that she can't dance like this anymore, because it's clear this is exactly what she was meant to do.

"What? Giving up already?" she asks, stopping to catch her breath.

I shake my head. "No, I just really enjoy watching you dance."

She lets out a long sigh and sinks back onto the floor. I follow suit, settling beside her. We lean back, shoulders almost touching, and take in the city lights stretching out before us. The air is cool against our skin, and even as we try to catch our breath, a comfortable silence settles between us for a moment.

"That's the first time I've danced since the accident," she whispers.

I want to say I'm surprised, but I'm not. Anyone in her place would've reacted the same way. Deep down, I already knew that. All I really wanted was to get her to dance, to have fun, to see that she can still enjoy it without performing.

"How was it?" I ask.

"Amazing."

I stare at her as the city fades, and all I see is her mouth, soft and unsure. For a second, I think about kissing her. But just for a second, and I don't move. Because she's still healing, and I am too. So, I lay back instead, arms behind my head, and stare up at the stars pretending to shine through the city haze. Jules lies down next to me, close, but not touching. And in this moment, that's enough.

Chapter Nine

Jules

I feel like I'm going to be sick. I've never been this nervous before in my life when visiting my brother. It took me an extra thirty minutes to get here because I kept thinking about turning around, making up some excuse about feeling ill. With how queasy I actually feel, it wouldn't have been a lie.

And that would be the only truth I'd tell him this visit. All day I've been preparing for this conversation, rehearsing every word in my head. Lying isn't the plan, but I'm not ready to tell him about my career change or anything else yet. This visit is about him, about being a good sister and helping where I can.

When he texted me to get together, I originally said my typical maybe, which we both know means no. He followed up the text with needing my help. Apparently, he has a new roommate. Well, just a buddy staying with him until he gets back on his feet. He didn't tell me much, but he said he could really use me as a buffer to them hanging out tonight, and that his buddy could use a friend as he doesn't have anyone else.

Oh, and there came a warning too. He didn't say as much, but he basically said he's off-limits. Apparently, he's a big flirt and playboy, so I need to be careful. It makes me laugh that my brother thinks I would fall for that. What he doesn't know is that I'm starting to really like a coworker, technically my boss, at a job he has no idea I even have.

I groan as I stand outside his apartment door. Do I really need to do this? Ugh. I shake my head and knock before I back out. It's going to be fine. I've never met this friend before, so I can just keep the conversation about him. Honestly, if he wasn't there as a buffer, I'm pretty sure I would've said no to coming over tonight.

My brother's piercing blue eyes shine behind his rectangular black glasses, and his large grin greets me as he opens the door.

"Jules!" he says, pulling me into a hug.

"Eric, it's good to see you," I say, patting his back as a sign he can let me go now.

"What? I can't hug my sister, who has been avoiding me for the past couple of months?" he asks, giving me his famous guilt-trip face.

"I'm sorry. I've just been so busy, but I'm here now," I say, feeling the guilt he's tossing my way.

"Well, come on in. My roommate, Jake, will be out in a minute." He's basically pushing me inside like he's afraid I'm going to bolt any second.

At the mention of the name Jake, my stomach does a flip. At least his name will be easy to remember since I'm currently crushing on a Jake. Though, wouldn't it be funny if it were my Jake? I laugh to myself. Yeah, that'd be funny.

I place my purse and shoes by the front door and head toward the couch. Before I can sit, the guest bedroom door opens. I watch as a very familiar man comes walking out.

No. No. No! Oh my God, no. It is not funny. This isn't funny at all. I was joking. Oh my God, I was just joking. No!

"Hey!" Jake says excitedly, just as surprised as I am.

I stare at him wide-eyed and shake my head subtly. No, it can't be my Jake. I can't let my brother know that I know him because then he's going to ask how. Then I have to tell him I work with him and how we met and how I'm no longer dancing and, oh my God, this can't be happening right now.

Jake continues to walk toward me and holds out his hand. "I'm Jake."

I let out the breath I was holding in, and I thank God Jake got the hint. I take a moment to process what's happening and finally take his hand to shake it.

"I'm Jules. Nice to meet you," I say, our hands bouncing up and down a few too many times.

We're both staring into each other's eyes, trying to figure out what comes next. He clearly understood the assignment, but how are we supposed to pretend like we don't know each other? We know too much about each other. He knows everything about me!

"Alright, dinner is ready," Eric says as he literally pulls Jake away from me.

Jake laughs, and Eric leans in and hisses, "She's off-limits."

Jake puts his hands up in surrender, grinning. Once Eric's back is turned, Jake winks at me and heads to the table.

I close my eyes and take a deep breath. "I need to go to the bathroom."

I don't wait for a response as I race into the bathroom and slam the door behind me. I close my eyes trying to steady my breathing and calm down. I've got this. Everything's going to be fine. Once I can think clearly again, I look around the bathroom to realize this must be Jake's bathroom. Well, that's not awkward at all.

He must have just showered because the towel hanging on the wall looks damp, and it smells like him in here. I take another deep breath, breathing in his scent. He does smell good... Ugh, what is wrong with me? Get out of here!

Reaching for the door handle, it hits me that it would look suspicious if I walked out without actually using the bathroom. Both of them are close enough to hear the flush and the water running, so I go through the motions. The toilet flushes, and I pretend I just went. After counting to ten, I turn on the faucet and wash my hands since we're about to eat. When I look around for a hand towel to dry them, there isn't one in sight.

The only towel in the bathroom is the one hanging on the wall that Jake clearly just used when he got out of the shower. Why does this always happen to me? This is the awkward moment where I debate using that towel or just wiping my hands on my shirt. Typically, I would fling my wrists to air dry my hands and then wipe the excess off on my shirt, but this is Jake. There is something wrong with me, but I really want to use his towel. So, I do. And now I feel like a creep.

Not wasting another second thinking about it, I leave the bathroom and take a seat at the table with them. Chinese food is set out all over the table, so I plate one scoop of everything. I love Chinese food, so typically I'd eat more, but my nerves are ridiculous right now. I know I'm not going to be able to eat much.

"Don't tell me you're on some weird dancer diet," my brother says with a worried look.

I take a bite of my food. "Nope."

He still looks worried. "You look like you've lost weight since the last time I've seen you."

I try to keep my voice even. "I've been working really hard."

Alright, see, I've got this. Sometimes dancers work hard and burn a lot more calories than they eat, so weight loss isn't uncommon. I didn't lie though, because I just said I've been working really hard, which I have been. Just not at the job that he thinks I'm working. The weight loss is probably also because I didn't eat for a while, and I'm not training anymore. I'm sure I'm gradually losing some muscle.

"I just worry about you. I hope you're taking care of your-self," he says.

Pushing the guilt aside again, I reply, "Of course." I turn to Jake to change the subject. "So how do you know each other?"

I watch Jake's reaction, which is a little weird. It's like he doesn't want to say, or he's just so nervous about slipping up that he doesn't know what to say.

Eric chimes in. "We met through a mutual friend."

The way he says that is weird. "How long have you known each other?" I ask.

"A few years," Jake finally answers.

A few years? That's interesting. I look back toward Eric. "How come you've never mentioned him?"

Eric shrugs. "We weren't close."

"Did you live in Georgia?" I turn back to Jake.

If they met a few years ago, it would've had to of been in Georgia. Eric hadn't left the state much, and he was still with his ex-fiancée, who I'm not a fan of. I only met her twice, and she seemed nice at first, but clearly, I misjudged her.

"Nope, I've lived in New York my entire life," Jake replies, shoving a big bite of chicken in his mouth.

The tension in this room is insane right now. I don't know if there's something they aren't telling me or if it's just because of the secrets Jake and I are currently sharing. Clearly, there are secrets all around tonight. As much as I want to push more to figure it out, I'm going to drop it. It's only fair since I'm not going to be spilling any of mine tonight.

"So, tell me how work's going," I say, continuing the conversation with Eric.

This was another one of my plans. I'm not going to leave any room for questions about me. I know they are going to happen, but if I notice even a little bit of silence or an opportunity for him to sneak one in, I'm going to make sure to fill it first.

"It's work. Long hours and boring," he states.

Well, I was really hoping he'd talk a little longer than that, but that's fine, I can keep going.

I look toward Jake. "What do you do for a living, Jake?"

He gives me the most devious grin, and I can't help but smile. He's gorgeous, and just like that, the butterflies in my stomach are back, attacking with full force. This whole situation is messed up, and I can't believe it's happening.

"I work at a hotel," he says.

I give him the same little devious smile back. "Oh yeah? What do you do at the hotel?"

"I'm the housekeeping manager."

I take another bite of sweet and sour chicken before continuing. "I'm sure all the housekeeping ladies love you as their manager."

He laughs out loud. "Yes, you could say that. There's one in particular that has caught my attention though."

Jake's staring at me with heat in his eyes. What the hell is that? I grab my napkin and wipe my mouth to keep the little smile from being seen along with the blush creeping up on my cheeks.

We continue eating our food, and the conversation keeps flowing, exactly like this. While it was awkward at first and I was nervous, Jake made it easy. Somehow, he always seems to know the right thing to say or do. He knows when he needs to be serious, but then he knows when I need him to be silly. I'm not going to lie, I think the more time I spend with Jake, the danger of falling for him increases.

Chapter Ten

• • • • • • • • •

Jake

Holy shit. I can't believe that Jules is Eric's sister. This thing with Jules just got a whole new added complication. When I walked out of my room to see her standing by the couch, I had to do a double take. At first, I thought that maybe I found her doppelgänger, but my mind caught up fast, and the things they told me about each other added up quickly.

Jules has been avoiding Eric because she doesn't want him to know about her career-ending injury. Eric invited her over under the pretense of helping me out. I had no idea he did that until a few minutes before she got here. He told me exactly what he texted her about how he needs her as a buffer and that I have no friends and could use one. Obviously, I had to agree to it because the man is letting me crash at his place.

Regardless, I had no idea that it would be Jules walking through that door. So, when Eric basically threatened me to stay away from his sister before she got here, I didn't think that it would be a problem, considering I'm starting to feel something for Jules. Yeah, that's the stupid situation that I'm currently in.

"I really appreciate you coming over tonight, Jules. We need to get together again soon," Eric says as he hugs her goodbye.

I walk up close to her and shake her hand. "It was great meeting you. I never would've guessed you were related. You're beautiful and look nothing like this ogre."

That's a fucking lie. In fact, that's lie number twenty tonight. So much lying. Now that I know they're related, I don't know how I didn't put it together myself. They have the same eyes, the same hair color, same complexion. Damn, they look really similar. The sense of familiarity when I first met her makes a lot of sense now.

She blushes as she pulls her hand away. "Thanks. It was good to meet you too. Good night!"

I watch her walk down the hallway until Eric closes the door and stares at me.

"What?" I ask.

He shakes his head. "Off. Limits."

I pat him on the shoulder and laugh. "I heard you the first five times."

"So, what are you doing tonight?" Eric asks.

I look at the time and realize that it's later than I thought. "I have a buddy coming to pick me up to hang out."

"Club?" he asks.

"Yeah, I think so. He's always vague about the details."

"Well, hope you have fun tonight. You know you're welcome to bring someone back here if you want. It's your place too now. I'm not going to be a cockblock," he states.

I laugh. "Thanks man, but I'm really not looking for any of that right now. I need to get my life in order."

"Wow."

"What?" I ask.

"I just never thought I would hear that Jake is putting girls on hold," he says seriously.

I shrug my shoulders and stay silent. Sometimes I wonder how I got such a reputation and whether it's truer than I realize. Everyone seems to think I've slept with a hundred girls. In high school, I did have a few, but most I just hung out with. A lot of them would lie and say we'd been together when we hadn't. I never corrected the rumors and, honestly, even played into them with jokes.

Once I got to college, I had several one-night stands before Everly and I had our friend's with benefits relationship. I turned to drugs and alcohol more than I'd like to admit, which contributed to poor decisions. After Everly though, there hasn't been a single girl. I've been to clubs, bars, and on vacation, but I just couldn't bring myself to do it. Not only was I just not feeling it with anyone, but I didn't want to do that to girls anymore. After Everly broke it off with me, and I realized we'd never be anything, it hurt like hell. I never wanted to make any girl feel like that when I wasn't willing to have more with them. It did more damage to me than I'll ever admit. Only Rowen knows about it. Regardless, I guess I've let people think that about me for so long that they think it's who I am.

My phone buzzes with a text, breaking me out of my thoughts.

Rowen

Outside.

He's always to the point. I grab my wallet from the counter and head down, jumping into Rowen's car.

"Where are we heading?" I ask, looking him over.

Once again, he's in disguise and looks nothing like himself. I get that he wants to ensure no one finds out who he is, but that must be exhausting.

He looks me over. "I see you haven't been wearing a hat and glasses."

I roll my eyes. "I don't even own a hat right now. Besides, this is a huge city, and I rarely go out. The odds of one of them seeing me are low."

"And if they do?" he asks.

I grin. "I run."

He shakes his head. "You're not very good at this."

"At what?"

"Hiding out. It's only a matter of time before you're caught," he states.

I shrug my shoulders. "Maybe."

He doesn't say anything else as he drives, and I look out the window. It's dark outside as it's late. I'm actually pretty exhausted and not wanting to stay out long, but Rowen insisted that I go out with him tonight. I really have a hard time telling people no.

We pull up at a familiar club, and he parks the car. He's about to get out when I stop him. "Rowen, we can't be here."

He looks over at me with his hand on the handle. "Why not?"

I shake my head. "This is Asher's club. He'll tell Everly I'm here."

"He won't if you tell him not to," he says.

"I really don't want to see him," I groan.

"We're going," he demands.

My heart pounds in my chest as I try to decide what to do. I don't want to say no to Rowen, but I also don't want to go in there. Asher is fine, but I really don't feel like seeing him right now. Rowen's right. He won't say anything to Everly if I tell him not to, I think. Even so, I'm not ready to see anyone from my past, be it someone I don't know that well or not.

Rowen opens the car door and yanks me out. Jesus, when did he get so strong? I stumble out of the car and onto my feet. Once I'm standing straight, he closes the car door and locks it. Great. I guess that's his way of ensuring that I go inside rather than staying out here in the cold.

The bouncer lets us into the club, and we immediately sit at the bar. Rowen orders us some beers.

"How have you been?" he asks.

"Fine," I state back because that's the truth.

"Just fine?"

I nod. "I haven't had time to sit and think much. I'm just surviving at this point."

He takes a swig of his beer. "That's what I was afraid of."

"What do you mean?"

He shakes his head. "Jake, you can't just keep going through the motions and pretending like everything's okay."

"I can," I mutter.

He places his hand on my shoulder. "Come on, man. You know that's not healthy for anyone, especially you. Why don't we talk things through?"

"No," I state sternly.

He sighs and downs the rest of his beer, ordering another. I didn't come out here to have a heart to heart with him. I had a feeling this might be the reason he called me to come out, but I was hoping it wasn't. Again, I love the guy, but he can be too pushy.

We're silent for a while, listening to the club music and watching the couples on the dance floor grind against each other. I'm surprised no girls have come up to hit on either of us. Usually by now there's one or two hanging around. My eyes also keep darting around the room looking for Asher, but thankfully I haven't spotted him. Maybe he's not working tonight.

"Well, would you look who it is." A hand lands on my shoulder, and I jump.

Jesus. Turning to look, I find Asher, who has a hand on both Rowen and my shoulders. Shit. How did he sneak up on me like that? I've been trying to keep an eye out for him.

"Asher! How's it going?" Rowen stands, giving him a hug and a pat on the back.

"Things have been great. What about you, Rowen?" he asks, smiling back at him.

Did he just call him Rowen? I definitely heard Asher call him by his real name. My heart squeezes in my chest with... jealousy? Damn. I thought I was the only one who knew him by his real name. I wonder how much Asher knows about him.

After exchanging a few words, Asher looks over at me with concern. "Jake, where have you been?"

I shrug my shoulders. "I've been around."

He shakes his head. "Everly's been worried about you."

My heart rate picks up again. This is exactly what I didn't want to happen. Why did Rowen bring me here? He knew we would run into Asher. What's his endgame? Why did I let him drag me in?

"Yeah, I'm sorry, but I don't want her to know I was here," I state seriously.

He nods. "Come on. Both of you come sit with me."

He leads us over to a private booth in the corner of the room. It's a lot quieter over here, and we can't see anything else going on in the club. Asher sits on one side, and I sit on the other, scooting in further so Rowen can sit.

"I'm going to hit the bathroom. I'll be back in a minute," he states.

Mother fucker. This was the plan all along. What the fuck is he thinking?

I finish off my beer and realize a new one has arrived at the end of the table. When did that get there? I eye it, and Asher pushes it over to me.

"Get what you want. It's all on me tonight," he says.

"Thanks," I mumble and gulp down half this beer as well.

"What's going on, Jake?" he looks at me again with the same concern as earlier.

Ah crap. I hate talking to Asher. I don't know what it is about him, but it's impossible not to tell him things. It's even more impossible to tell him a lie. Half the time I'm trying to say one thing to him, but something completely different comes out of my mouth. I swear he's magic. He's also like the most perfect-looking human being, with all symmetrical features. I'm not gay by any means, but the man is gorgeous. He has dark brown, reddish hair that goes past his ears. Asher hasn't changed his hairstyle since I've known him. His eyes are a shade of green that seems so rare, and it's impossible to look away from him.

Asher and Everly go back many years. She met him here when the five of us completed our summer bucket list before senior year of high school. He owns the place, along with half of New York. The guy is young, and he looks like he doesn't age. I have no idea how he got to where he is today, but I'm pretty sure he's richer than all my family and friends put together.

I finally get out of my thoughts and answer him. "I've just been trying to figure out my life."

"Is it because of Everly?" he asks.

I laugh and chug the rest of my beer. "No. I mean, she was a small part of it, but it's not her…"

Well, here it is. That stare he gives. I'm telling you he's magic. All my reservations about telling him what's going on go out the window, and I spill everything. I mean, fucking everything, from my father disowning me to Jules. When I finally finish talking, it's been almost an hour. Where the hell is Rowen?

"That's… a lot," he replies.

"Yeah…" I sigh.

"Look, Jake. I know you have a lot going on right now to figure out, but I don't think keeping your family and friends at a distance is what's best for them or you. There's something holding you back. What is it?" he asks.

I think for a long moment. What is holding me back? "I guess I just don't want to be a burden to any of them."

He shakes his head. "Nah, that's not all. There's something deeper." He stares at me like he's willing me to dig deep.

I lean back and sigh. "I don't want them to think of me as a fuck-up. Everyone has always had an image of me that isn't true, and now this is. Now I'm actually the fuck-up everyone thinks I am."

Asher frowns. "You're anything but a fuck-up, Jake."

I shrug my shoulders and look away. "Maybe, but no one really needs me around. They're better off without me right now."

"No!" Asher shouts and grips my wrist hard, bringing my attention back to him. "Don't ever say that again. For as long as I've known Everly, there's one person that she always talks about every single time I see her, and that's you, Jake. You held her together when she was in Georgia. You mean everything to her, and I don't know your brother as well as I know her, but I know that he needs you too. What about Ben? You've been best friends since you were kids. Did you know I've seen each and every one of them in here either drunk or filled with grief since you've been gone? Even James."

Asher's still holding onto my right hand, so my left hand raises to press into my eyes that are springing fucking leaks. I can't be weak and cry here, in front of him. This is stupid. What the fuck am I doing here?

I'm startled as he turns over my hand and pulls up my sleeve. I quickly try to pull it back down, but it's too late. My eyes meet his.

"Don't you dare do that to her, Jake."

He squeezes my wrist so tight that it hurts. I want to pull away, but I honestly don't have the energy.

"I won't," I whisper.

He pulls down my sleeve and lets my wrist go. "She lost one friend to suicide. It'll destroy her if she loses another."

"I'm not suicidal, Asher. I'm just... fuck, I don't know," I state, feeling angry now.

"When did you do that?" he asks, nodding toward my arm.

I try to look away, but damn it, I'm telling you he's impossible to ignore. "After she broke it off."

He sits back and rubs his hand through his hair and stares me in the eyes again. "You still love her?"

I shake my head. "I'll always love her. She's my best friend, but no. I don't have feelings for her like that anymore."

He nods. "Good. I think Jules is going to be good for you."

I smile. "Yeah, me too."

We sit and talk for a little longer until finally Rowen comes back. He's been gone almost two hours. We thank Asher for the drinks, and I thank him for the talk, even though I didn't really want it.

Just as we're walking away, Asher stops me. "Jake."

"Yeah?" I turn around, and he's right in my face.

"You ever need anything or need to talk, you come to me. If you kill yourself, I'll bring you back and kill you myself," he says in a joking way, but ominously serious.

I huff a laugh. "Yeah, okay."

Fuck. Coming from him, I feel like he could and would do it.

Rowen and I make it back out to the car, and I feel... a lot lighter.

"Was this your plan for tonight?" I ask.

He shrugs. "I was hoping. Asher has a way of getting people to open up and reveal their secrets."

I sit forward and laugh. "Right?! I always say the dude is magic. You can't even lie to the man. It's insane."

Rowen laughs too. "I swear you're right. How do you think he knows my real name?"

I sit back and sigh. That makes me feel a little better too about Asher knowing his name. It's stupid to be jealous of that.

"Hey Rowen," I say.

"Yeah?"

"Thanks."

"Anytime," he replies, and we drive the rest of the way in silence.

CHAPTER ELEVEN

JAKE

All the talk about Everly with Asher has made me dream about her for the past two nights. I hate knowing that I'm causing her pain right now, especially when she's pregnant. I'll figure my life out soon so I can see her again. The dreams have been about the same thing... me fucking up with her. As I continue to lie in bed, my mind wanders back to the day I ruined everything we could've been.

Ben and I are playing darts as I keep glancing over at Everly. She's sitting on the couch, talking with two girls that she met today at the party. Ashley and Lauren are good girls. Everly will fit right in with them. As much as I want to go hang out with her and sit her on my lap again, I know she needs this time to make friends before school starts. We'll have plenty of time later.

Ben's beating me in darts because I can't stop taking glances at Everly. I saw her looking over here a couple of times, but her gaze keeps wandering toward James. I'm trying really hard not to get jealous, but I've always figured she has a thing for him. He's a lot harder to read, though, and I'm not sure that he feels the same way. He'd be stupid not to.

"Hey Jake," Jenny, a girl from school, says behind me.

"Hey," I reply, smiling back at her.

Jenny and I rarely talk, and when we do, I know it's usually not a good thing. I found her in the janitor's closet one day at school crying. Using a hall pass, I was heading to the bathroom when I heard someone whimpering. I opened the door to check it out and found her. Apparently, her boyfriend just broke up with her because he told her she was too fat. If she wanted to have a chance with him again, she'd need to lose the weight. My skin still boils from that prick's comments.

Anyway, I used my usual charm and flirting to make her feel better. We both walked out of the closet together, and because she was with me, the students in the hall who saw us assumed we just had a quickie. We didn't correct them because what's the point?

I can see in her eyes that something just happened. Guiding her toward the corner, I lean in close so she can tell me what's going on without anyone else hearing. I keep a smile fixed on my face, a mask to keep attention away from us.

"What's going on?" I ask.

She takes a deep breath before saying, "I dressed up tonight to show Jackson how much weight I've lost... and he turned me down."

Keeping the smile on my face is really hard right now as my blood is boiling. Before I can say anything, Ben interrupts us with a hand on my shoulder. I give him a questioning look, trying to understand what the face he's giving me is about.

Ben clears his throat. "Let's finish our game, Jake."

"Yeah, give me just a minute," I respond, but he keeps his hand on my shoulder.

"I think it's best if we go now." He nods toward Everly.

Ah crap. Does Ben think that I'm flirting with this girl? Will Everly think that? No, I can't imagine she would think I'm capable of doing that to her.

"Seriously, Ben, just a minute," I say, trying to convey that this is important.

He shakes his head and walks off toward Everly. Hopefully, I can resolve this quickly and head over there as well.

"Sorry, I shouldn't have come to you," she says while turning to back away.

I catch her arm and lean in even closer while looking to the other side of the room, finding her jerk of an ex staring at us.

"He's right there watching. Let's make him jealous," I say.

"How?"

"Just keep smiling and laugh with me," I say.

She nods, and I laugh loudly with her joining in. Our laughs must be convincing because he looks angry.

I lean over to whisper in her ear. "I think it worked. Though he's a jerk and doesn't deserve you."

She blushes. I lean back and see Everly and Ben walking out the door. Looking toward her friends on the couch and their expressions as they stare at me, shows me she's upset. Crap.

"Let's go," I say, grabbing her hand and walking out the door and down toward the bedrooms.

"Thank you, Jake. I appreciate what you've done for me. You're so sweet."

I nod. I feel bad about her situation and would love to help her further, but now I'm concerned about Everly. Her new friends come out of the room and head straight down the stairs.

"I'm sorry I can't help more right now, but I need to go find my girlfriend," I say, giving her an apologetic smile.

Her eyes widen. "You have a girlfriend? I didn't know... she didn't see us, did she?"

I rub my hands through my hair. "Yeah, I think she did. I just want to make sure she's alright."

As I'm walking away, she comes up behind me. "I'll come with you and explain everything to her if needed."

Just as we're passing the room we came out of, Jenny's douche of an ex comes barreling out.

"What the fuck, Jenny?" he asks, looking between the both of us.

"What?" She straightens.

"I just turned you down and you're already with someone else?" He looks at me and scoffs. "Not just someone, but Jake, really?"

I step in front of her. "I think it's time to go, Jackson."

"Yeah, you're right. Let's take this outside," he says.

I inwardly sigh and roll my eyes. I don't have time for this, but I'm not about to leave Jenny with this asshole. "Let's go."

All three of us walk out the front door and off to the side where no one can see us, covered in trees. I really hope this isn't going where I think it's going.

"Jake, you should go. This has nothing to do with you," Jenny says, pleading with me.

I laugh. "I'm not leaving you alone with him."

Before I know what's happening, Jackson is slamming me up against a tree. He gets in my face, and he's angry. I know the guy's a jerk, but I've never seen this side of him before.

"You fucking my girl?" he asks through gritted teeth.

"Jackson! Let him go!" Jenny yells.

"Stay out of this, Jenny!" he yells back without looking at her.

I'm not sure what she's doing because I'm not taking my eyes off him. I don't like to fight. Physically, that is, but I will if I have to.

"Answer the question," he spits.

"Why does it matter? She's not yours. You're the one that broke up with her," I spit back.

"I'm going to mess up your face, pretty boy. I know your reputation. When I heard you two hooked up at school, I didn't believe it was true. Now I see it is."

"What do you want, Jackson?" I ask, keeping my cool.

"You to stay away from my girl."

I shake my head. "She's. Not. Yours."

His nostrils flare, and he grabs my hair to pull my head back to look up at him. He's taller than I am, so he has to lean down a little to get directly in my face. I'm on guard and ready to end this if he takes it too far, but I'm not going to throw the first punch.

"Stay. Away. From. Her!" he growls in my face.

"Jackson, stop it! Let him go! You broke up with me, remember? Why do you want me anyway when I'm too fat for you?" she asks.

He stares at me as if he's debating punching me. I'm ready for it. To my surprise, he just shoves me back and lets go, turning to Jenny.

They start talking, but I'm distracted by seeing Everly and James walk out of the house as her security guard, Declan, pulls up in front of her. Crap! I quickly turn toward Jenny and Jackson, and he seems to have calmed down a bit. I just need like five seconds.

I race back toward the house, but Everly is already getting into the car with Declan about to close the door. "Everly, wait!" I yell.

James stands in front of me, placing his hand on my chest, shaking his head at me. I want to punch him in the face right now, but Declan closes the door and drives off quickly with her. Fuck!

"Seriously, Jake?" James looks at me disappointed and angry.

"Seriously, James?" I ask back.

"You had an amazing girl right in front of you and you went off with someone else?"

My heart sinks. James thinks that too? He's not even giving me an opportunity to explain. He already has in his head what happened, so what's the point?

"Whatever," I say, pushing his hand off me.

I glance back to find Jenny and jerkface making out against the house now. All that for nothing.

I pull out my phone to text Stan to pick me up. My heart stops again to find a missed text from Everly, asking where I was. I wish I would've seen it, so I could've told her something. Anything. I pull out my phone and call her over and over again until Stan pulls up to get me. Once I'm in the car, I shoot off text after text, praying she'll answer.

I shake my head to get out of that memory. Of course she didn't respond to my calls or texts. I didn't sleep at all that night, just wanting to explain what happened. The next morning when she agreed to meet with me, I knew it was over between us the moment she came outside to talk. She already had in her mind that what she saw was the truth, that I was flirting with another girl. She said as much in her texts beforehand. So, I just went along with it. What was the point? I just admitted to her what she thought she saw and apologized. I knew I wasn't going to win her back, especially after her confession of loving James.

The only thing I ever cleared up was that I didn't sleep with Jenny. Knowing Everly thought I could do that to her destroyed me. Falling apart inside, I do what I've always done. Pretending becomes second nature. I become exactly who everyone expects me to be. Flirting with her, trying to win her back, I pretended I'd be fine with a friends-with-benefits setup. Even kissing her was part of the act, hoping she'd believe it. I stayed the same happy, flirty guy everyone knows because that is who I'm supposed to be. That is all anyone ever sees. The guy who jokes, flirts, and makes everyone else feel lighter is not the one who is slowly breaking while smiling through it.

I rub my hand over my face and force myself to get out of bed. I think about Jules and how I'll be able to see her in a couple of hours at work and at lunch. Surprisingly, she hasn't texted me at all about the other night. I know that I should be heeding Eric's warnings and staying away from her, but I don't know that I can. I really want to talk to Eric about it, but I can't do that either because then I'd have to betray her.

Regardless, I decide to send her a quick text. I've fucked up everything with everyone else. I don't want to with her too.

> It's been a long weekend without you. I can't wait to see you today.

She doesn't respond immediately, so I toss my phone on my bed before heading to the shower to get ready for the day.

CHAPTER TWELVE

JULES

When I get out of the shower, I find a text from Jake, a.k.a Onion. We haven't talked at all this weekend about what happened at Eric's place. I wanted to text him so many times, but I didn't know what to say. I didn't know how he was feeling or whether he would reveal to Eric what he knew about me. How close are my brother and Jake?

My heart practically jumps out of my chest as I read his message. He... missed me? Really? Then why didn't he text me sooner? Maybe he feels the same way, but he's tangled up in everything that happened, and now I don't know what to think.

I don't know what is going on with us, but I'm finding it harder and harder to keep him out of my thoughts. Jake is charming, sweet, and basically perfect in every way. I find myself drawn to him and wanting to get to know everything about him. I wanted to get my life figured out before attempting anything with someone, but I'm thinking of throwing that out the window for him. The main issue now is my brother. Clearly, he doesn't think Jake would be good for me, and I can't even imagine why.

Texting him back feels like the right move. Everything else can wait. For now, I just want to feel good again, whole, alive. Somehow, being around Jake makes that possible.

> I missed you too. See you for lunch today?

Jake responds immediately.

I'm looking forward to it.

I can't help but feel giddy at these texts. I feel like I'm in high school all over again with a boy giving me attention and asking me out. Everything is messed up in my life, but Jake makes me happy. I'm not going to give that up easily.

My phone is ringing, and it's my mom. A sigh escapes me as I debate whether to answer. I'm getting ready for work, though she doesn't even know about that. Finally, I decide it's time to pick up one of her calls.

"Hello?" I answer.

"Jules! Finally! You've been ignoring my calls for weeks!" she exclaims.

The guilt rises inside me. I love both of my parents, but I can't fathom telling them the truth yet... that everything they sacrificed for me and my career has been for nothing.

"I'm sorry, I've just been so busy," I explain.

"I bet you're working really hard! We can't wait to come see your first show. When is it again?" she asks.

Well crap. "It's not for a while, but I'll text you the dates soon."

"Alright, well regardless, we're coming to New York this weekend, and we hope you can squeeze us in for a dinner," she says.

My heart races even faster. No, I can't do this yet. I can't.

"Oh, wow, that sounds nice. I'm sure Eric will be excited to see you. I'll do my best," I say.

"You have to have a spare moment. We could even do breakfast, whatever works for you, sweetie," she says calmly, but I know there's no getting out of this.

"Yeah, okay. I'll look at my schedule."

"Anything new going on with you?" she asks.

Oh yeah, everything is new. My dream career is gone, and now I'm stuck cleaning hotel rooms just to scrape by. This job only came my way because I lied about dating a friend of the boss. By the time my shift ends, I'm completely drained, barely holding myself together.

I guess I take too long to reply because she asks excitedly, "It's a boy, isn't it?! Oh, Jules, tell me all about him!"

I groan. "Mom, I really have to get going."

"Oh fine! But you'd better bring him to dinner or whatever we do. I won't take no for an answer," she says.

Shit. I could probably ask Jake to pretend to be my boyfriend, but Eric will be there. There's no way I can bring him. Ugh. I'll have to figure this out. Pretending like I have a boyfriend is the perfect opportunity to keep everything off my career. I'm just not ready to tell them yet.

"When are you meeting up with Eric?" I ask.

"We're flying in Friday night and staying at a hotel. We'll see Eric on Saturday. He's going to take us sightseeing, and then he leaves Sunday afternoon for a business trip, and we head back Monday."

I sigh in relief. This could work. We could do dinner Sunday night, and Eric wouldn't be the wiser. I just have to make sure that they don't meet Jake before the dinner.

"I think Sunday night dinner will work for me. I'll double-check and let you know," I say.

"Wonderful! I can't wait to meet this boy of yours. Have a good day, darling. Love you!"

"Bye mom. Love you," I say, hanging up the phone and tossing it on the bed.

Well, this is going to be fun.

Lunch time takes forever to get here. I had some crazy rooms to clean, but thankfully none of them were as bad as the one Jake and I did together our first week. I really hope I never have a room as bad as that again.

As I enter the lobby, Jake is leaning against the wall by the fireplace. I catch his attention immediately as I walk in, and he moves to greet me.

"Hey," he says casually.

"Hey," I respond back, grinning like an idiot.

"The usual?" he asks.

I nod. Jake and I tried a couple of restaurants around, but we found one that we both really like down the street. It has pretty much everything you can think of. In the mood for breakfast foods? They've got eggs and pancakes. Want lunch? Here's a good wrap. Dinner? Have a juicy steak. The best part is it's cheap. Eating out for lunch every day can get expensive, but it's worth it since I get to do it with Jake. Though he's yet to let me buy a meal.

As we're seated at a table, one of the usual waitresses comes over. "How are you two today?" she asks.

"Great. How are you?" Jake replies with his flirty smile.

She basically giggles and blushes as she replies. Seriously?

"Good. The usual?" she asks, looking between the two of us.

"Yes, please," we both say at the same time.

When she walks off, I roll my eyes.

"What?" Jake asks.

"Does every girl you meet fall head over heels for you?" I ask sarcastically.

He laughs. "I don't know… you tell me. Did you fall head over heels for me?"

Well, I walked right into that one.

I tap my chin as if I'm thinking over a response. I am. "Not at first."

He freezes. I think I actually surprised him with that answer. "So, you have now?"

I shrug my shoulders as the waitress comes over with our waters and begins talking for a minute. I ask her how she's doing in school, even though I honestly couldn't care less. She's a nice girl, but she flirts with Jake a little too much for my liking.

While waiting for our food, I decide to drop the bomb about the phone call I had earlier with my mom.

"What are you doing Sunday night?" I ask, hopeful that he's free.

He's staring at me with those gorgeous eyes and grinning. "I don't have any plans yet, why?"

Ugh, he looks so smug. He could get any girl he wants, and I can tell he knows it.

"I have a favor to ask…" I trail off.

"What is it?"

Alright, here goes nothing. "Since we're doing the whole fake dating and all… would you be willing to continue this charade Sunday night with my parents?"

He looks at me for a minute, like he's contemplating it. "So, you want me to pretend to be your boyfriend in front of your parents?"

I nod, and I know I'm blushing.

This time he taps his chin like he's thinking it over and smirks. Bastard.

"Can I ask why?" he asks.

"Does it matter?" I ask back.

He shrugs. "Not really. I'm just curious."

Sighing, I explain, "My mom called me this morning telling me they'll be in town. I was avoiding telling her about everything, and she assumed I had a boyfriend, which I didn't correct her. So now I got roped into bringing said boyfriend to dinner. Eric is on a business trip on Sunday, so I figured that's the perfect time for the dinner, without him there. Oh, and you have to make sure you avoid them as his roommate."

Man, I'm so sick of him just staring at me. I want to know what he's thinking.

He shrugs. "Yeah, sure. I can pretend to be your boyfriend for your parents."

"Really?"

He laughs. "Yeah."

I shake my head. "There's nothing you want in return? I feel like you've been dragged into this whole fake relationship solely because of me with Tristan and now my parents. I owe you."

Our food arrives, and Jake doesn't pay the server any attention this time. Once she leaves, I start digging into my food because it's the only thing I can think of to help with the awk-wardness of all this.

"Nope. You don't owe me anything. I like hanging out with you, so it works," he says, taking a bite of his own food.

Well, that was really sweet. I don't know what I did to deserve such a great guy like Jake to come into my life. I just wish I was in a better place so I wouldn't feel like such a burden, and really be able to concentrate on having a boyfriend.

When lunch is over, he opens the door for me, like the gentleman he is. Once we're outside, he slips his hand into mine. My heart practically stops, and the butterflies in my stomach are doing somersaults, twisting and turning like they own the place.

"What are you doing?" I gasp, looking up at him.

"I figured we should start practicing. You know, since we're boyfriend and girlfriend." He winks at me.

Well, that just melted me into the ground. I don't know how I'm going to survive pretending to be his girlfriend for much longer.

CHAPTER THIRTEEN

JAKE

"Hey man, I forgot to tell you my parents are coming over in a bit," Eric drops the bomb on me.

I stop mid-chew of my breakfast. "Define a bit."

He looks at the clock and cringes. "Like fifteen minutes."

Shit. I quickly stand and throw my plate in the sink, not even caring that I still have half my breakfast on there.

I'm almost to my bedroom when Eric laughs. "You don't have to get out of here. They know I have a roommate."

I chuckle. "Ah, nah. You reminded me I need to be somewhere. I'm going to hit the gym and then head out."

He looks at me skeptically before saying, "Alright, well I'll see you tonight."

"Sounds good. So, where are they staying?" I ask.

"Down the street at a hotel."

Great, they could be here any second. I don't waste time with small talk. My hands shove clothes, my toothbrush, and basically my whole life into my gym bag as panic rises. It's fine. I can get out of here quickly once I change into workout clothes. The plan is simple: hit the gym downstairs, shower, and figure out the rest from there. Maybe I'll grab a hotel for the night just to be safe. Coming home isn't an option if they decide to hang out. Crap, I didn't think this through when I agreed to it with Jules.

"See you later." I send a quick wave to Eric as I walk out the door.

Once I make it to the gym, I relax. I'm not really in the mood to work out, especially since I just ate. I sit on the bench and pull out my phone to text Jules.

I watch the little dots appear moments after my text.

Jules

Come to my place to hang.

It's okay. I'll be fine.

Jules

It's not fair you're kicked out because of me. Come over. I'm not busy and we need to discuss what being my fake boyfriend looks like.

You sure?

Jules

Yes. See you soon.

I look around the empty gym and debate for a moment. Should I go to her place to hang out? She's not wrong that we should figure out some things before meeting with her parents. They're going to want to know where we met, how we met, and how long we've been together.

After a long walk and a subway ride, I finally reach Jules' apartment. She's sitting on the front steps, like she's been waiting for me. My chest tightens, and a smile spreads across my face as I move closer. She hasn't noticed me yet. Leaning back on her hands, she lets her eyes drift over the sky, and her hair whips around her face in the wind. She looks impossibly beautiful, and I can't stop thinking about how lucky I am that she's here, just like this.

"Hey," I say, startling her out of her trance.

"Oh, hey." She gets up and leads me inside.

I follow behind her and up the steps to her apartment. After all this walking and carrying my heavy bag, I'm thankful I didn't work out. I have no idea why I threw so much in my bag to go out. I guess I wasn't sure what I would do after everything and wanted to be prepared in case I had to avoid going back to Eric's place until tomorrow when he leaves for his trip.

We step into her apartment, and right away I notice how much cleaner it is compared to the last time I was here. There's still a little clutter on the counters and coffee table, but everything looks tidier, more intentional. No clothes tossed across the couch, no trash lying around. Even the carpet looks freshly vacuumed. And it smells good.

"Did you clean just for me?" I joke.

She laughs. "Well I couldn't let you see my messy side twice. I have to impress my fake boyfriend when I know he's coming over."

I kick off my shoes at her front door and place my duffle down next to them. Walking further in, I make my way to the wall where the television is. I didn't get much of a chance last time to explore her apartment, so I do it now. Looking at the pictures on the wall, I find one of her and Eric that looks like it was taken a few years ago. There are also a couple of professional dancing photos of herself scattered through and another of her, Eric, and her parents. Eric and Jules both look just like their mom.

I study the photo next to it, which is of her in a ballet outfit doing a pose. She's absolutely stunning. She looks serious in the picture, but I can see in her eyes just how much she enjoys it. My heart sinks thinking about how she just recently lost what she loves the most in life. She acts as if she's holding up so well. It makes me wonder if that's what people see when they look at me.

"You done snooping?" she asks, bringing over a glass of water for me.

"Thanks," I say, grabbing it from her, and our fingers brush.

She clears her throat. "Did you have any plans today?"

I shake my head. "Not at all. It was going to be a lazy day."

She smiles. "Me too."

Taking a sip of my water, I ask, "So what does the mysterious Jules do on her lazy days?"

She laughs. "Do you really want to know?"

Grinning, I answer, "Of course."

"Well, sometimes I'll read, but my favorite thing to do is binge-watch something on Netflix."

Well, that's... completely normal. I didn't expect her to actually sit down and be lazy. She doesn't seem like the type that can just sit. More like she always needs to be doing something.

"Don't let me ruin your day. I'll just sit and watch with you."

We move toward the couch, and she sits down first. I pause, debating whether I should keep a little distance or slide in right beside her. The truth is, I want to be close... closer than I probably should be. The urge to pull her against me catches me off guard. I can't remember the last time I wanted to cuddle, but right now, the idea sounds amazing.

So, I drop down right beside her, close enough that our bodies almost touch. She doesn't comment, just grabs the remote and flicks on the TV.

"What do you like to watch?" she asks nervously.

I shrug my shoulders. "I'm down for anything. Watch whatever you would've before I came over."

She has a wide grin on her face before she starts scrolling through Netflix. I have a feeling she's looking for something to make me regret not choosing. When she stops scrolling and finally lands on something, I laugh. I knew that's what she was doing, but what she doesn't know is that I actually enjoy this show.

"I've been binging *Gilmore Girls* again lately. It's my favorite," she says as she presses play.

"Me too," I state with a smirk.

"What? Really?" she asks, surprised.

I nod. "Yep. Also, I never expected the ending of the new ones that came out. They'd better make more so we can find out what happens."

She stares at me as if I have three heads.

"What?" I ask.

Shaking her head, she responds, "I just never would've thought you were a *Gilmore Girls* fan."

We both lean back to get comfortable as the show starts, and I place my arm around her shoulder. I thought about placing it on the back of the couch, but I figured I'd be bold and go for the shoulder to see what she does. I can back off if she wants me to.

"What are you doing?" she whispers.

I lean over to whisper in her ear. "Isn't this what couples do? I figured we should start practicing before I meet your parents tomorrow."

She sighs and leans into me, resting her head on my shoulder. I have to say I didn't expect that, but I really like it.

"Yeah, you're right," she says, cuddling even closer.

Neither of us moves or even seems to breathe for what feels like hours. Sitting here with her like this is far more comfortable than I ever expected. Too comfortable. Like we've somehow slipped into real-couple territory.

After the third episode, Jules finally sits up and faces me. "We should probably talk about things for tomorrow's dinner."

I nod. "Yeah, probably a good idea."

Her hand is fidgeting with the bottom of her shirt as she talks. "I was thinking we'd stick to the truth as much as we can. We can tell them we met a few weeks ago and the whole subway story with you helping me. Instead of bringing me to get a job, we can just say we went out to eat and hit it off from there."

Halfway through her speaking, I grab her hand and hold it still. Our fingers are entwined, and she hasn't pulled away from me.

I lean closer to her. "Sounds good."

I catch the way she swallows hard, her eyes flicking down to my lips before darting back up. Shit. I wish she hadn't done that, because now I know she wants more too. She wants me to kiss her, and damn, I hate admitting it, but I've been dying to taste those soft pink lips since the day we started working together.

I'm losing what little control I have when it comes to this girl. She makes me feel something I haven't felt in a long time, and God, I want it more than I should. The timing couldn't be worse for either of us, and we both know we shouldn't go there. But right now, I can't bring myself to care.

I continue to slowly lean closer, to see if she stops me. She doesn't. When I'm about to go for it, she says, "Jake..."

I pull back just a little and stare into her eyes. "It would sell it more if we kissed while out with your parents. Maybe we should practice that?"

Seriously? What am I, ten? I have to use the pretense of our fake relationship to kiss this girl rather than just saying I really want to fucking kiss you, Jules?

She nods and closes the distance herself. Her lips meet mine tentatively as we figure out what this means to both of us. How long should this go on? I want to continue kissing her forever, but does she want the same? Or is she doing this solely as practice, like I said?

She changes the intensity of the kiss, and I follow, grabbing onto the back of her head. She leans back on the couch and pulls me with her, on top of her. Placing my hand on her cheek, I continue to kiss her as she squeezes me to her with her hand on the back of my head and on my back. She moans as I run my hand through her hair and deepen the kiss with our tongues tangling together.

I don't know how long we kiss as it feels like forever. Every part of me wants to take it further, but I don't. My hands stay in safe, respectable places, and so do hers. As much as I hate it, I finally pull back and meet her eyes. She looks like she wants exactly what I do, but we both know we shouldn't. We can't. It won't do either of us any good.

I sit back on the couch and run my hand through my hair, clearing my throat. "I think we'll be convincing with the kissing."

She chuckles. "I think so."

We both sit on the couch in awkward silence until she finally stands up. "Do you want lunch? I can throw in a frozen pizza or something."

"Sure, sounds great," I say as she's already in the kitchen preparing it.

I pull out my phone to look busy, but it's a lie. I can't stop thinking about that kiss. I can't stop thinking about her. How the hell am I supposed to get either of them out of my head? Part of me doesn't want to. Part of me knows I never will.

Chapter Fourteen

Jules

Jake and I walk hand in hand into the restaurant to meet my parents. I'm thankful for the physical contact with him again. After yesterday's kiss, neither of us said a word about it, and we kept our distance from each other. We binged a few more episodes of *Gilmore Girls*, talked a little, and even played a few card games. We didn't touch once.

I offered him to spend the night because I texted Eric asking how things were going with our parents, and he said they were still hanging out at his place. Jake didn't want to accept at first, but eventually I convinced him he could just crash on the couch, and it wouldn't be a big deal.

I was wrong. It was a big deal. Sleep barely came as I thought about him in the other room and the kiss we shared. That kiss was the best I've ever had. The urge to sneak into the living room and jump him was almost irresistible. It would have been a mistake, given everything going on in our lives, but I just wanted to feel something amazing for once. At one point, I went to the kitchen for water in the middle of the night, wearing only a baggy T-shirt and panties. I'm pretty sure he was awake and saw me, but he quickly closed his eyes to pretend he didn't. Part of me hoped it might spark something in him, but I know it was for the best that he didn't.

We find my parents already sitting at a booth, and they stand up when they spot us heading their way. I let go of Jake's hand to hug both of them. Jake shakes their hands, introduces himself, and scoots all the way inside of the booth so I can sit on the outside. He didn't even ask because he already knows I can't stand the feeling of being trapped in a booth.

Jake immediately places his hand on my leg and rubs it with his thumb as the waitress comes and takes our drink order. Once that's settled, my mom takes the opportunity to start the grilling. Her eyes are beaming as she looks at Jake.

"So, tell me how you two met," she asks, waiting for a romantic story.

Jake flashes me a grin. Oh no. Here it comes.

"Oh, it was great. She fell for me, literally. Right on the sidewalk," he says deadpan.

I roll my eyes and mumble, "Tripped over air."

"She was on the ground, and I thought, wow, an angel in distress, I have to help. It was very romantic, and there were pigeons," he says with his grin widening.

I should've known Jake couldn't just go with a simple story. I knew he'd have to embellish it, but I let him tell it anyway.

"There were no pigeons," I state.

He pats my leg and says, "I'm telling it my way."

My mom beams. "That's so cute! A meet-cute!"

My father decides it's his turn to chime in. "What do you do for a living, Jake?"

At this point, our waitress comes back with our drinks and takes our food order. Jake continues to stroke my leg where his hand is placed on my thigh. It has moved over significantly, so his long fingers are basically under my leg while his thumb is on my inner thigh. It's pure torture, and I haven't been this turned on by a simple touch… well, ever. I try to peek over at him to see if he's doing this intentionally, but he's looking straight ahead at my parents as they order like he's not doing a damn thing.

Once the waitress leaves our table, Jake answers my father. "I work in hotel management."

Dad looks like he's filing that information in the back of his head before he continues. "What about your parents? Do they live around here?"

Jake nods, and his hand stills at having to talk about his parents. "They do, and so does my brother."

"What does your brother do?" My father continues with the interrogation.

I know Jake doesn't want to talk about his family right now, and I really should put a stop to it, but I can't bring myself to. It's helping keep the topic off me for as long as we can, and hopefully I can avoid talking much about my nonexistent dance career.

"He owns his own financial company."

Dad's face lights up. "That's wonderful. Did you know that Jules' brother is an accountant? He loves all that financial stuff."

He nods, and my mother finally chimes in. "Have you met Eric yet?"

Jake takes a quick look at me, and I know it's time for me to come into the conversation to save him. We didn't really talk about how we would answer questions like this.

"Eric's met him, but not under the pretense of being my boyfriend," I state.

Dad chuckles. "Yeah, I'm not sure how he'd feel. Jake and Eric seem completely different."

The topic stays on Jake for a while longer until the food comes. We're mostly silent and enjoying our meals until my mom can't take the silence anymore.

"Jules, we want to hear all about your new role and how it's going," she says as I stop breathing.

I knew they would want every little detail. It was expected, but no response had been prepared. Thinking about it made me uneasy. All I could do was hope that somehow they had forgotten the last thing they heard, that I had landed a role on Broadway.

"Intense. I've just been going nonstop, and I'm exhausted."

I pray they leave it at that, but I know they won't. They're my parents. They have been so supportive of my dreams since I was a little girl and gave up so much for me to pursue them. Jake's hand squeezes my leg to comfort me. I place my hand on top of his, and he moves from holding my leg to my hand seamlessly.

"You've always been such a hard worker. You're not overdoing your leg, are you?" my father asks.

I debate getting up and running out of here right now. How suspicious would they be if I did that? I haven't even told Jake about that yet. In high school, I hurt the same leg, and the doctors cautioned against overdoing it and permanently damaging it. How do I even respond to this? If I say anything other than, I fucked up my leg and my career ended, then it'll be an outright lie. I can feel my breathing quicken, and panic is creeping in. Why didn't I think of answers to these kinds of questions?

Jake reaches for his glass of water and ends up knocking it all over the table and both of us. He lunges for the napkin next to me and somehow knocks my drink over too.

"Geez, two for one. Whoops. Come on, let me help you dry up. So sorry," he says, scooting out of the booth after me.

Neither of us looks back at my parents' reactions as he places his arm around my shoulder, leading me toward the restrooms. Thankfully, it's a one-person bathroom, so we both step in, and Jake locks the door behind us.

"Sorry about that," he says as he grabs a few paper towels to dry me off.

"Did you do that on purpose?" I ask.

He doesn't stop patting me with the paper towels as he responds. "You looked like you were panicking, and that was an impossible question to answer. I figured you could use a distraction and a breather."

He did that for me? Knocking over a glass at dinner is embarrassing enough, but twice, just to get us out of there? He sat through my parents' interrogation, answering questions about his family and his life that he clearly didn't want to. And he did all of it for me?

"Jake..." I say, grabbing his hands to keep him from continuing to dry me off.

"What?" He stops and straightens, staring at me.

I don't say anything as I grab the back of his neck and pull him down for a kiss. He doesn't resist and grabs the back of my head to deepen it. The kiss is hard and hungry, with tongues clashing and both of us moaning. God, I need this man so bad. I know this is all fake, but at this moment, it doesn't feel that way.

After at least a full minute, I pull back, breaking the kiss reluctantly.

"Thank you," I whisper, staring into his eyes.

"Anytime," he responds, clearing his throat.

We leave the bathroom together, both still drenched. I'm soaked more from that kiss than from the water he spilled. I can't let myself think about it though, not now, as I'm about to sit back down with my parents.

When we arrive back at the table, it's been cleaned up, and the seat is dry.

"The server cleaned the mess," my mother states.

I slide into the booth after Jake and say, "Oh great. Thanks. I'm still pretty wet."

Jake laughs. "Sorry about that. I think her clumsiness rubs off on me."

I smack him on the shoulder. "Hey! I'm not that clumsy."

"We literally met because you tripped on nothing," he grins at me.

I cross my arms. "There was a crack in the sidewalk!"

He raises a brow. "You acted like it was a sinkhole."

"I was surprised! Gravity betrayed me."

Jake leans in with his eyes gleaming. "Gravity seems to be betraying you a lot lately. You've lost a fight with a revolving door, swivel chair, and coffee lid… all this week."

I gasp. "That chair was spinning on its own. It was a setup!"

My parents' laughter brings us both back to reality. I'm blushing as I stare at them, and my mom's looking at us in a way I've never seen before.

"You two are perfect for each other," she says.

My dad clears his throat. "I never thought Jules would find anyone who could handle her. I'm glad to see I was wrong."

The rest of the night goes exactly like this. My parents never bring up my dancing again, other than stating they can't wait to see my first show. Jake helped quickly steer conversations away from dancing and onto everything else. My parents loved him.

Once we left, Jake ordered an Uber for me to ensure I got home safely. Eric's apartment was close by, since we went to a restaurant close to my parents' hotel. I wanted to invite him back to my place again, but I didn't think that was a good idea.

Jake and I are complicated, and I didn't want to add to that complication.

Chapter Fifteen

Jake

Ignoring the chatter around me, I smile down at my phone as I scroll through the texts Jules and I have been sharing the past week. That night at her apartment and dinner with her parents changed everything between us. While we haven't talked about making anything official yet, we've been actively flirting and really getting to know each other. I think at the moment it's easier for both of us to do everything under the pretense of our fake relationship. If we don't make anything official, then we're not going behind Eric's back, and no one gets hurt. We also haven't discussed either of the kisses we shared.

Rowen plops down in the seat at the bar next to me. Once again, he's in a disguise that looks nothing like himself. I don't think I'll ever get used to it.

"You're late," I say, taking a sip of my whiskey.

He smirks. "She's getting clumsy."

"Ah, that's great," I say and leave it at that.

He doesn't like talking about business outside his home, so he usually talks in code like that. Anyone listening in would have no idea what we're talking about. This means that he's getting close to finally catching the person that's been hacking into Bash's company's accounts. It never takes this long for Rowen to find someone, so this chick must be really good.

"Everything still running smoothly?" he asks, watching my expression.

I grin. "It's running great."

He studies me for a second before responding. "It's the girl, isn't it?"

I laugh. "How'd you guess?"

He shakes his head. "Well, you're still in the same position you were before, so it has to be the girl. I'm happy for you. Jules seems great, and she's clean."

I shake my head. Of course, Rowen would look into her. I'm thankful he did, though, so I don't have to worry about anything. You never know who people might pretend to be when they think they can get to your money. Something Jules still doesn't know about... well, not that I have any money to worry about right now, anyway.

Rowen stiffens beside me and grabs a bar menu, which he never does. He places it right in front of his face, acting like he's studying it.

"Act like you don't know me," he whispers without his lips even moving.

I continue to drink my beer and watch the television in front of me, waiting for further instructions.

"I told you it was just a matter of time if you weren't in disguise. You're on your own. Three O'clock," he says in a low voice.

I casually turn my head as if I'm stretching my neck to look in that direction. I immediately make eye contact with James. Fuck!

James stands from his seat, and I go to bolt out the front door, but his head of security, Ryder, is blocking my path. Thankfully, we're in my buddy's bar, so I know it like the back of my hand. I bolt through the kitchen and out the back door. Just as the door closes behind me, I'm body-slammed into the wall from behind.

I turn to find Declan, Everly's security guy, as the one pinning me. My mind races in fifty directions. Do I surrender or do I fight? I'm not ready for this, so my answer comes easily.

"Sorry, Declan," I say as I knee him in the stomach and head-butt him.

He groans but doesn't let go. "Fuck, Jake!"

We grapple, and I manage to deliver several more strikes before he retaliates. This lasts for another minute until Ryder makes his way to us and grabs hold of me. Damn it. I'm a good fighter, but there's no way I can fight these two off without actually hurting them. My fight or flight is kicking in, and the fight has won. I take a couple of blows at Ryder, and all three of us struggle against the wall.

A calm voice cuts through, making me pause. "Everly needs you, Jake."

At those four words, all the fight drains out of me. Ryder and Declan don't loosen their grip as they guide me to the parked car and shove me into the back seat. James slides in beside me, while Declan and Ryder take the front. Both of their eyes stay fixed on me.

Taking a deep breath, I run my hand through my hair. "Fancy seeing you guys here. What's up?"

James looks at me with furrowed brows, and both Declan and Ryder look at me like they want to get a few more punches in. Okay, yeah, I don't blame them. I shouldn't have fought them.

"Where the fuck have you been?" James' calm manner turns quickly to anger.

I shrug my shoulders. "Around."

James shakes his head. "Why are you running?"

"Need to get my exercise in," I state with a smirk.

James groans and literally pulls at his hair. "Jake! This isn't funny. What the fuck is going on?"

I shrug my shoulders again.

"We're not leaving this car until we talk," James says.

Crossing my arms, I lean back against the door, getting comfortable. "That's cool. It's a nice car."

"Fucking hell," Ryder joins in.

I want to laugh, but I know it'll piss them off even more. I'm surprised I'm not as upset as I thought I would be with them finding me. Maybe it's because I knew without the disguises, like Rowen said, I'd be found. Or maybe deep down I wanted to be found. I don't know.

I lock eyes with Declan. The longer we stare at each other, the weaker I get. Damn it. The guy loves Everly as much as we do, and he doesn't need to speak for me to know what he's saying. I've hurt Everly by disappearing.

"I'm sorry," I whisper, not breaking the eye contact.

Declan nods. "Come home, Jake."

I shake my head and laugh. "I have no home."

James looks more concerned now than angry. "What do you mean?"

Sighing, I respond, "My father disowned me and took everything, and I mean everything. My apartment's gone, my stuff, my car, my phone, my damn underwear. There's nothing to come back to."

"We'll get back to that. Tell me what happened," James demands.

"He didn't agree with the way I lived and decided it was time to get rid of his good-for-nothing son. I'm surprised he didn't do it sooner."

"Jake…" James starts, but I cut him off.

"Nah, James, it's fine. I'm sorry I went MIA on you guys. I just… I needed time to figure things out," I say as I look out the window.

James sighs. "Jake, why didn't you come to us? You know you could have stayed with us, and I could've given you a job."

I laugh. "Yeah, I could have. I know that, but it's fucking embarrassing, okay? I'm always such a fuck-up, and I'm sick of relying on everyone else to help me out. I need to do this on my own."

James, Declan, and Ryder all look at each other for a moment as the car is silent. I'm antsy and want to get out of here.

"Alright, I talked. Can I go now, please?" I ask, hoping they'll unlock the car door.

James clears his throat. "Everly has been worried sick about you. She's not sleeping and barely eating. She's not the only one. Bash and Ben are spending all their time looking for you too. It's been a damn month, Jake... we thought you were dead."

My heart squeezes as the guilt settles in. "I thought my father would've told you guys I was on vacation," I whisper.

James shakes his head. "After the second week, your father became as worried as the rest of us. He came clean, saying he kicked you out, but now he couldn't find you and he thought you'd be back by now."

I laugh. "My old man worried about me? That's funny, James."

"I'm not joking, Jake. Everyone's been fucking worried about you. It's time to come home. We can figure it out together."

Have they really all been worrying about me? The guilt is sinking in even deeper now. Here I've been getting all cozy with Jules and comfortable in my new life without thinking much about them while they've all been searching for me. If my dad told Bash he didn't know where I was and was worried too, then I know Bash hasn't been sleeping or doing anything but trying to find me because that's what I would do if the roles were reversed. How did I let it go on this long?

"I didn't think anyone would care," I whisper.

"Well, we all do. So, are you coming home? Come stay with us. Everly's throwing a gender reveal in a few weeks, and she needs you there," he pleads.

I think about it for a moment. I could just go back with them right now and pretend this past month didn't happen. Even if my father won't give me my position back, I know I'll get one with Bash or James. James and I went years barely speaking to each other because of Everly. He forgave me, and we're back to being best friends again, like we all were as kids. I don't want to mess that up again.

If I do that though, then what comes of Jules and me? And Eric? Eric and I hang out every weekend and have formed a real friendship too. Jules and I are in a weird spot, but I can't imagine leaving without figuring out where we stand. I know if I head back now, things will never work out between us. No, I can't head back yet. I have to figure things out first.

"I can't. Not yet," I say.

"Jake..." James begins, but I interrupt him again.

"No, listen, James. I have some things I need to figure out first, but I promise I'll come back. I'll be there for the gender reveal. Tell Everly whatever you need to make her feel better. Just give me a little more time," I bargain.

"I can't just let you leave, Jake. Everly won't feel better until I bring you home," he states seriously.

Fuck. I knew he wouldn't just let me leave again without a fight. As shitty as I feel for making Everly worry, I can't go back. I pull the card that I've been holding onto since high school and never intended to use.

"I'm calling in the favor, James. You have to let me leave and not follow. I promised you I'll come back and be there for the reveal. I won't break the promise," I state, watching for his reaction.

It takes him a moment to realize what favor I'm calling in, and his face squeezes tight before he rubs his face like he's angry. Either angry with me or the memory that favor brings up. Yeah, it was a shitty way to win the favor, but it's still valid. We were dumb the summer before Everly came to stay with us for the year and made a bet about which one of us she'd end up sleeping with. The winner got a favor from all the others. I won the bet, and it's not something I'm proud of. I never intended to call in any of their favors, and I haven't, until now.

"Fine, but you better show up for the reveal. Do you have a new phone?" he asks.

I nod. "I'll give it to you, but promise me you won't give it to anyone else. Text me the information for the party, and I'll be there."

I pull out my phone and text James. Never thought James would be the first person from my old life I'd text. I figured it would be Everly, Bash, or Ben. Soon enough, they'll all have this number too. Hopefully, I can figure things out with my life before then.

"Does Bash know that you found me?" I ask.

"No... I didn't want to get his hopes up," James says.

"Okay, yeah. Just tell him I'll see him soon, okay?"

James relaxes but looks like he has something more to say. We're silent, and I wait for whatever it is, but it never comes. Instead, I hear the door unlock, so I open it.

"Jake," James stops me.

"Yeah?"

"Are you okay? Do you need anything? Money?" he asks.

I laugh. "I've survived a month with nothing. I'm fine."

All three of them look at me with concern, so I get out as quickly as I can and slam the door on them. Their car doesn't move as I walk down the street and around the corner. I lean against the wall and take a deep breath, letting it out along with my nerves from the entire exchange. My hands are literally shaking. I continue my walk back home to Eric's place, where I'll probably spend the rest of the weekend figuring out my next move. It's time for me to go home and back to reality. I just hope Jules will come with me.

Chapter Sixteen

Jules

I'm so relieved this is the last room I have to clean this week. My whole body aches, and I'm sick to death of scrubbing after people who treat hotel rooms like trash cans. I'm tired of the smell, the stains, the little reminders that no one respects the person cleaning up their mess. All I want is to go home, collapse into my bed, and disappear under the covers until the world stops demanding anything from me. That's been my life lately. Nights and weekends lost to staring at the ceiling, numb and hollow, because I have nowhere to go and no one expecting me. People would probably call it depression. They'd be right. I'm fucking depressed, and the worst part is, I don't even know how to claw my way out anymore.

"I fucking hate rich people!" I shout as I'm scrubbing the vomit off a wall.

"Wow, what did rich people do to you?" I turn to find Jake leaning against the open hotel room door, watching me.

I finish scrubbing the spot and throw my rag into the bucket dramatically hard. "They have absolutely no cares about anyone in the world. They think we're all their maids and can do whatever they want."

Jake's smile turns to concern quickly as he walks toward me. "Is everything okay?"

My damn eyes burn, tears threatening to spill. I'm angry. No, furious. And I don't even know why it is hitting me so hard right now. Well, I do know why, but it feels ridiculous that it is all bubbling up at this moment, out of nowhere, like I have been holding a match too close to gasoline and finally set myself on fire.

"You want the truth?" I ask.

"Always," he says sincerely.

"No, I'm not okay. I'm not fucking okay," I shout and throw my arms up in the air.

I hurry and take the cleaning supplies out of the room so I can be finished and go home. A small part of me feels bad for blowing up like this, but I've reached my limit. I've bottled up everything for so long, it was bound to come out at some point. I just wish it could've waited another hour when I was back at home, not with Jake standing right here.

Jake comes up behind me, spinning me to face him. I know the tears are falling, and I don't care at this moment.

He pulls me into a hug and says, "Finish putting this up, and I'll be right back."

I nod and do what he says. After I get everything put back where it belongs, I wash up and wait for Jake. It doesn't take long for him to return, and a little bit of my anger has faded. Just a little.

"Come on," he says, grabbing my hand, leading me up to the top floor and into one of the executive suites.

"What are we doing?" I ask.

"I called Tristan and asked for a room for the night," he says like it's a normal favor to ask for.

"He gave you an executive suite for free?!"

He grins and shrugs. "Benefits of being buddies with the owner."

I shake my head and plop myself down on the couch with my face in my hands. I don't even know what to say right now. Jake sits down beside me and rests his arm around my shoulders.

"Talk to me, Jules."

I sigh and look at him. The anger has faded a good bit, but it's still there. "I don't want you to see this side of me, Jake."

"I want to see every side of you. You're angry, and that's okay. Let it out. I'm here," he says like he really means it.

Maybe I should. Maybe I need to finally let out my anger and just get everything off my chest. I have no idea where we stand right now, but if he sees this side of me and runs, then so be it. At least then I'll know.

I stand up and let it all out. "Alright, you want the truth? I'm so fucking angry, Jake. I'm angry with the world and at myself. My life is so off course, and I don't even know what to do. All the dreams I clung to, the ones I had bled for, were snatched away before I even had a chance to live them. Now I'm just going through the motions of cleaning up other people's shit, literally! This is the worst job I've ever had, and I hate it. I'm barely surviving and have no money. Everything I make goes to rent, medical bills, student loans, and other expenses. Some weeks I wonder how I'm even going to eat... I hate my life!"

I take a deep breath and let it out. Wow, that felt so good. So good to finally put it all out there and tell someone. Tell myself.

I get the courage to glance at Jake. He's staring at me, and I can't read his expression. Does he think I'm crazy? Is he going to run and say, nice knowing you? I really wish he'd say something. Anything.

Jake stands and walks toward me. He pulls me into a hug, and I lean into him. I wasn't expecting that.

"You'll get there, Jules, I promise. You'll get a job you love, and things will start getting better," he whispers in my ear.

I don't know why, but that breaks me. I cry and sob into his chest for what feels like hours. He doesn't say a word, just holds me and lets me release it all. When I'm finally drained, I realize we're sitting on the couch. I don't know how we got here, and a wave of embarrassment washes over me. I don't want to lift my head from his chest, not yet, not when I feel this exposed and raw.

"I'll get a bath started for you, okay?" Jake asks as I finally lift my head.

I nod, and he gets up, heading to the bathroom. I pull out my phone to find a text from my brother.

Bro

> Hey! I'm back in town. Want to do dinner this weekend?

As much as I want to respond, I don't. I know that I'm going to have to tell him everything soon, but I'm not ready for it. The next time I see him, I have to tell him.

Jake comes back out and helps me up, leading me to the bathroom. "I'm going to order some room service for dinner, so take your time."

He closes the door, and I quickly undress, sinking into the large jacuzzi bathtub. It feels so good, and I never want to leave it. What a life this must be to have the type of money to afford this. I can't believe Jake got us this room for the whole night. I was going to leave after having my breakdown, but now I'm thinking, why not stay the whole night? Enjoy a nice comfortable bed tonight and shower in the morning.

I must have dozed off because Jake wakes me as he knocks on the door. "Hey, dinner is here, and I have some clothes for you. Do you want me to bring them in?"

He has clothes for me? I try to quickly decide what I want him to do. Do I risk having him see me naked in the tub? All the bubbles have cleared out, and you can fully see everything.

"I'll close my eyes," he shouts through the door.

"Okay!"

Really? Okay is all that I could think to say? As the door opens, I cover myself just in case. Jake does what he says and covers his eyes as he walks in. I can't help but smile at how cute he is. He places them on the counter and quickly heads back out of the bathroom and closes the door.

"Thank you!" I yell.

After getting out of the tub, I dry off and get dressed. I don't know where he got these clothes, but they fit perfectly. He brought some underwear, a sports bra, a T-shirt, and leggings. They are really comfortable.

I exit the bathroom to find Jake setting out a bunch of food, drinks, and desserts.

"You ordered all of this?" I ask, taking in the large spread of food that we could never eat in one night.

He shrugs. "Tristan said to order whatever we wanted. It's on him."

"Wow. You guys must be pretty close," I say, wanting to know a little more about Jake.

"Not really. We became buddies a few years ago. He's a great guy," he says.

He picks up some food to eat, so I do the same. Everything looks so good, but I pick up the quesadilla because that's my favorite.

"Oh, where did you get the clothes?" I ask with my mouth half full.

He smiles. "I texted a friend for a favor to bring some."

"You have a lot of friends," I state.

"I was pretty popular in high school and college."

"That's right. You were a frat boy," I say as I take another bite.

He doesn't respond, and we continue eating in silence. I'm not sure exactly how we're supposed to proceed. I just had a complete meltdown in front of him, and all he's done is take care of me without a single word. I'm trying not to read too much into it, but I know I'm falling for him. We're both so broken, though. How could something like this possibly work?

Jake breaks the silence after we finish eating. "We have the room for the night. Do you want me to leave so you can get a break for a night?"

Really? He got this amazing room from his friend for the night and he's offering to leave? Who is this guy?

"No. I want you to stay," I say.

He nods. "I can take the couch. It looks more comfortable than the bed I sleep in at your brother's."

We both laugh, but there's tension hanging in the air with what he just said. My brother, that's right. My brother would be so mad right now if he knew I was with Jake. But why? Why was he so adamant that I stay away from him?

I shake my head. "The bed is big enough for both of us. I mean, if you want."

His eyes narrow at me, and he holds his breath. I don't think he expected me to offer that. I didn't mean we would have sex... I just meant we could both sleep in the bed. Oh no. Does he think that's what I meant? Panic starts creeping in again.

"Okay, sure," he replies, like he's deep in thought.

We clean up the food, and head to the couch.

"Want to continue watching *Gilmore Girls*?" he asks.

"Absolutely." I grin and turn the TV on.

Once again, I find myself cuddled up against him, and it feels... so right. He hasn't said anything about the meltdown that I had earlier, and he's acting like it never happened. Maybe he'll want to talk more tomorrow, but I'm not going to think about it right now. I'm going to enjoy cuddling with him on the couch and watching my favorite show.

Chapter Seventeen

Jake

I lie awake thinking this was the worst decision I've ever made. Why did I agree to sleep in the same bed as Jules? We went to bed about an hour ago, and we're both facing away from each other. I'm pretty sure she's asleep, but I haven't been able to even close my eyes. It's been so many years since I've been with someone that my dick is about to explode. I was hard even before I got into bed with her. I had to take my pants off when she was in the bathroom and jump in bed before she came out.

I turn on my back because I can't take another second staring at this stupid wall. I'll give the ceiling another hour before I turn back to my side. Definitely not facing her though, especially since she's in nothing but that t-shirt and panties. I don't blame her for not wanting to wear pants to bed. I can't either.

"Are you awake?" Her whisper comes through the dark and startles me.

"Yep..." I groan.

She sighs and rolls over, facing me. I do the same and, damn it, I knew I shouldn't have. She's so fucking beautiful even in the dark. I haven't wanted a girl so badly since... well honestly, probably ever.

"This was a bad idea, wasn't it?" she asks quietly.

I laugh. "Yes, it was."

Her hand comes up from under the blanket, and she pushes the hair aside that fell in my face. Just that one little touch sends a signal to my dick, making it strain even harder. Didn't know that was possible at this point.

"I really like you, Jake," she says with a serious face.

I grin. "I really like you too, Jules."

She's quiet for a moment, but she doesn't take her hand off me. In fact, she scoots closer and drags her hand down my arm. Damn it. It's getting so much harder to keep my hands to myself.

Neither of us says anything as her hand continues its descent down my arm, over my hand, to my stomach... and then she reaches my dick, which is hard as a rock at this point. She wraps her hand around it, and I hiss.

"Jules..."

Her eyes meet mine as she continues to stroke it, scooting even closer. My chest tightens, and my pulse hammers in my ears. With her mouth just inches from mine, I can't take it anymore. I need her. I want to lose myself in her completely.

"I want to feel good for a night. I want to make you feel good... I want to forget the rest of the world exists," she says with her lips right up to mine, not quite touching.

"Then let's forget," I growl and break the distance.

I kiss her harder than I've ever kissed anyone before as I push her on her back and crawl on top of her. Her soft gasp sends a thrill through me, and suddenly nothing else exists. The world outside this room, the consequences, all of it disappears. It's just her and me, and I'm desperate. Taking her wrist, I force her to let go of me. I'm about to fucking explode, and my boxers are still on.

I hold both of her wrists in my hand, pinning them above her head as I continue to kiss her. I don't let go until I have to as I kiss down her neck, force her to sit up, and rip the shirt off over her head. Fuck, she doesn't even have a bra on. Only her panties remain, but that's quickly remedied as I yank them off and toss them to the floor.

I kiss down her jaw, tracing her neck with my lips, my teeth grazing lightly, and I feel her shiver under my touch. Every movement she makes, every sigh drives me crazier. I want to leave a mark, to make sure she knows she's mine, to burn this moment into memory, knowing this may only be for tonight. I know she's about to reach her limit, but I keep going.

"Jake..." she groans like she's in physical pain.

"What do you need, Jules? Tell me," I say as I continue kissing up her leg and reach her inner thigh again.

"I need your mouth on me," she breathes out.

I smirk and crawl back up so my lips are just over hers. "My mouth has been on you."

It's dark, but I can see her roll her eyes. I chuckle as I kiss her lips and then start my descent again, torturously slowly. She groans again.

"Tell me what you need, baby," I say, continuing the slow pace, dragging out this moment.

"I need you to eat me out, Jake. Now," she demands.

"As you wish," I say, lowering myself and throwing one of her legs over my shoulder.

I can tell she's not used to the dirty talk, so I'll give her this one. I don't waste any more time as I give her what she needs. I lick and suck for barely a minute before she's exploding around me. Her thighs clench together, squeezing my head as I continue. I continue even after she's done because I can't get enough of her. That wasn't enough. There's a hunger in me I haven't felt in years.

"Jake," she pulls on my hair, trying to get me to stop.

"Mmm... Baby, you taste so good, though," I say as I go a little longer.

She pushes my head away as she sits up. "It's my turn."

Pulling off my shirt and boxers, I ask, "What do you want to do?"

She stares me in the eye with confidence. "I either want you to come in my mouth or fuck me. Your choice."

Ugh, what an impossible choice. I've imagined fucking that pretty mouth too many times while jacking off lately, but fucking her sounds amazing too.

I groan. "I don't have a condom."

She thinks for a minute. "Are you clean? When was your last test?"

I nod. "I'm clean and it was years ago, but I haven't been with anyone since."

"What?" she asks, surprised.

I smirk and push her back down on the bed, hovering over her. "Are we going to talk about this now, or can I fuck you?"

She nods. "I'm clean and have an IUD."

I'm done waiting. I spread her legs and push into her. God, she feels so good. It's been so long, and I've never had sex without a condom. I feel like this is a stupid fucking mistake, but I can't control myself anymore. Every inch of me aches for her, every nerve screaming that I need more. I'd go insane if I couldn't be inside her right this second.

"Jules..."

"Jake..." she moans out my name.

It's only been a couple of minutes, but she's already coming, and the sensation of her squeezing my cock is about to send me over the edge.

I quickly pull out, pump my hand, and come all over her chest. Holy shit, I've never come that hard in my life, and seeing my cum all over her, claiming her, makes me never want to let her go. She's mine.

I'm panting with my chest heaving as I collapse on the bed beside her for a moment. Pulling myself together, I roll off the bed and head into the bathroom to grab a towel to clean her up. As I'm wiping everything off her chest, she's looking everywhere but at me. Did I just fuck everything up?

Once I finish, I ask, "Are you okay?"

She still doesn't look at me as she nods and says, "Yep."

Well, that's a lie. I throw the towel on the floor, not caring about it, and crawl on top of her again. I force her to look in my eyes.

"What's wrong?"

"Seriously, nothing. That was great," she says, still not convincing me.

I chuckle. "I'm not getting off you until you tell me what's going on in that head of yours."

She shakes her head.

"Jules..." I say seriously.

She sighs. "I was hoping just for a fun night to forget the world..."

"But?" I ask when she doesn't continue.

She looks away and back again. "I didn't expect... it to feel like that... with you."

Oh, thank fuck.

"Oh, Jules... are you falling for me?" I joke to lighten the mood.

Her face turns surprised as she slaps my arm. "Get off me, Jake."

I roll off her and laugh, and so does she.

After a minute of us settling down, I pull her close, still facing her. "I didn't expect it either. I want you, Jules."

"Really?" she asks, surprised.

And that surprises me. "What do you mean, really?"

She laughs. "What could you possibly like about me?"

"You're joking, right?" I ask seriously.

She stares at me, waiting for a response. What's not to like about her? She's perfect.

"Jules... you're smart, funny, kind, beautiful, and you like me for who I am. You don't judge me or make assumptions... You're fucking perfect, and I don't know how I got so lucky to be here with you tonight."

At first, she doesn't look like she believes me, but then she pulls me in for a kiss. It's tender and doesn't last more than a minute.

"Where does this leave us?" she asks.

I let out a deep breath. "I don't know. Let's take it a day at a time, okay?"

She nods. "Okay, yeah."

Neither of us says anything else as she cuddles into me and I hold her. Her breath evens out as she falls asleep, and I quickly follow.

Chapter Eighteen

Jules

I wake up with arms wrapped around me and a leg over my hip. It takes a moment to remember where I am and who I'm with. I grin as I recall everything that happened last night. Jake and I had sex. It wasn't meaningless sex. It was with someone I've gotten to know and really like. I've never had that before. It was amazing.

Jake stirs behind me, and I roll over to face him. He's already watching me, a smile tugging at his lips. God, he's hot. How does someone look that good in the morning, especially after the night we just had? His hair is a tousled mess, but somehow it only adds to his perfection.

"Good morning." His voice is rough, still heavy with sleep.

"Good morning," I smile as I answer.

He leans forward and kisses me. For a moment, I think he's going to try to have a repeat of last night, which I wouldn't object to. Instead, he pulls away and sits up on the bed.

"Do you want to get room service for breakfast?" Jake asks.

"Sure. I'm good with whatever," I shrug, trying to play it cool.

Jake picks up the phone and orders a pastry platter, some eggs, sausage, bacon, and coffee. It all sounds amazing.

I get up to head to the bathroom, and Jake stops me. "Oh, I put some toiletries in there for you. I grabbed them last night while you were sleeping."

Wow, I must've really passed out last night. I didn't hear him leave. I was thinking after hitting the bathroom I was going to do the same, but clearly, he's one step ahead of me.

"Thanks," I say as I close the bathroom door.

Looking in the mirror, a mess stares back at me. I wish I could look even half as good as Jake does when he wakes up in the morning. My teeth and hair get a quick brush, an attempt to look a little more presentable. Makeup would help, but I'll have to go without. So far, he hasn't complained, which has to mean I'm okay.

Once I'm finished in the bathroom, my phone buzzes on the end table. I walk over and see it's my brother calling. He doesn't usually call without sending a bunch of texts first, so I answer. Something in my gut tells me that something isn't right.

"Hello?" I answer.

"Jules, where are you?" he asks with concern in his voice.

"Huh?"

"I'm at your apartment, and you're not here. Where are you?" he asks again, and my stomach sinks.

"What are you doing at my apartment?" I ask back in an accusatory tone.

Jake is watching me at this point, and I sit down to keep myself calm.

Eric sighs. "I know you said you have Saturday mornings off from practice, so I came by to talk."

"What is there to talk about?" I ask again, impatiently.

"Jules! Where are you?"

"I slept over at a friend's last night," I say, which isn't a lie. Technically, Jake is still just a friend since we haven't put a label on it.

"Tell me where and I'll come get you. We really need to talk."

"Eric, I can't today. I'm busy."

Eric grows frustrated. "There was an eviction notice on your door, Juliet! What's going on?"

My heart sinks into my stomach. Shit. I meant to go to the office yesterday to give them more money and tell them my plan to catch up on payments. I completely forgot. How could I forget? And why did Eric have to pick this one day to come by?

I sigh. "It's fine, Eric. I have it under control."

"Jules. I'll stand outside your front door all day if you don't tell me what's going on," he says seriously.

My heart rate picks up. This is it. I need to tell Eric everything. He's not going to back down from this, but I'm not ready. Will I ever be ready?

"I'll be home this afternoon. Come back later?" I ask.

He groans. "Fine. I'll be back at four, and you better be here."

"I'll see you soon." I hang up the phone before he can say anything else.

"What happened?" Jake asks me with concern in his voice.

I take a deep breath and let it out. I'm trying to control my nerves and tears. "Eric stopped by my place and found an eviction notice on my door."

"Shit. Why was he at your place? And eviction notice?" Jake asks, concerned.

"The notice will be taken care of. Eric said he knew something was wrong and wanted to talk. Now he really knows... I have to tell him, Jake. I have to, and I don't want to."

Jake sits on the bed with me, holding me as I try to calm down and breathe normally. I knew the day would come when I'd have to come clean about everything, but I wasn't ready for it to be now.

"Do you want me to be with you when you tell him?" Jake offers.

"No... I'm not ready for him to know about us either, since he clearly doesn't want us together."

Jake groans. "Yeah..."

I sit back up and look Jake in the eyes. "Why doesn't he want us together, Jake?"

He shrugs. "I don't know. I figure it's because he only knows me as a flirt and a playboy."

My heart stops. "Playboy?"

I knew about the flirting because I've seen it firsthand. But it's never felt real. The more I watch him, the more I realize it isn't about attraction at all. He flirts to make people smile, to make them feel seen.

Rolling his eyes, he says, "Yeah. I seem to have gotten that image. I just never corrected the assumptions. I had a time where I went through a few girls, but nothing crazy. I haven't even been with a girl since meeting him."

"Seriously?" I ask in disbelief.

He laughs. "You were shocked last night too. Why is that?"

I wave my hand at him. "Because of all this. Look at you. You're gorgeous and sexy with this perfect body. I know there have to be hundreds of girls throwing themselves at you every week."

"Nah. If they are, then I don't notice. And right now, there's only one girl I notice," he says, winking at me.

I want to roll my eyes at him, but I don't. I haven't known Jake for that long, but he doesn't seem the type to say things like that and not mean it. He's smooth, but again, he just doesn't seem like he pulls this on girls. I still can't believe it's been years since he last had sex.

"So, what's your story, Jake? Why have you sworn off sex for so long?" I ask jokingly, but he turns serious.

He looks away for a moment, as if he's thinking about how to respond. "Honestly, I just didn't want the meaningless sex. The last person I was with I really liked, but she didn't feel the same about me. It hurt, and I didn't want to do that to anyone else. I promised myself I wouldn't have sex again until I found someone I could see being with. More than just sex, you know?"

Wow. I didn't expect him to actually answer the question, but I'm glad he did. My chest aches knowing he was hurt by someone in the past. The flicker of jealousy that rises is gone almost as quickly as it comes, replaced by the weight of everything else he said. He thinks he can be with me? I know we both have our issues, but would it be so bad to have each other to lean on and figure out all the shitty stuff with?

"So, you want to be with me, huh?" I joke, but it's a serious question.

Jake grins and grabs me, pushing me back on the bed while climbing on top of me. "You would latch onto that part."

He's tickling me while kissing me. I can't stop laughing. "Jake!"

"Yes, my love?" He stops tickling me but stays on top of me.

Did he just say "my love?" I shake that thought out of my head. It's just a term of endearment, nothing more.

I can't get that out of my head, though. "What are we?"

He's still on top of me and kisses me before asking, "What do you want us to be?"

"I want to be your girlfriend," I say seriously.

That grin reappears. "Fuck yes."

He kisses me again for another minute but eventually pulls away and rolls off me. I don't know what it is about this man, but he can make me forget everything wrong in the world. Somehow, he made me completely forget about having to talk to Eric tonight, but now that I'm remembering, I'm cringing at the thought.

"Everything is going to be okay. Eric loves you and is going to support you completely. He's not going to judge you or be upset you can't dance anymore," he says, holding my face in his hands.

I nod. "Yeah. You're right."

Jake thinks for a moment before sighing. "Tell you what. You do this, and I'll go see my brother tonight. Text me when you're done, and I'll come over if you want."

I smirk. "Look at us confronting our issues head-on."

He laughs. "Yeah, yeah. It has to happen at some point. Now that I have a girlfriend, I need to get my life in order."

Girlfriend. There's something about that word coming out of Jake's mouth. Girlfriend. I have a boyfriend. Knowing that Jake's my boyfriend gives me the courage I need to face everything to come.

Chapter Nineteen

JAKE

Standing outside my brother's apartment building, I wonder why the hell I ever told Jules I'd do this. My pulse is hammering, every beat loud enough I swear the people passing by can hear it. My stomach twists so hard I feel like I might puke right here on the sidewalk. My palms are damp, my throat tight, and the longer I stand here, the more the walls of this city feel like they're closing in.

It's just my brother. Just him. The same guy I've known my whole life. So why does it feel like I'm about to walk into a firing squad? Like the second that door opens, everything I've been trying to keep hidden is going to be ripped right out of me?

I groan just thinking about how this will go. Bash is going to be pissed at me for disappearing for a month, and honestly, he has every right to be. The guilt's already eating at me, but I know it'll be worse the second I see him. I've always been good at putting up a front, at pretending everything's fine so he doesn't see the demons clawing at me from the inside. Lately, though, they've been slipping through the cracks. I know he started to notice. That's why I had to get away. My father just handed me the excuse I needed.

With how long I've been standing here, people probably think I'm some kind of creep casing the place. Maybe even waiting to rob someone. And honestly, since I have no clue what I'm going to say to him, turning around sounds like the smarter option. I could walk away, pretend I never made it this far, and try again later.

"Jake," a familiar voice stops me from continuing away from the building.

Fuck. What did I expect? Wells is exceptional in security. That's exactly why Bash made him head of his. I wouldn't be surprised if he had some high-tech cameras set up to ping him the second my face showed up anywhere near this building. Okay, maybe not that far... but clearly, he saw me standing out here.

I suck in a deep breath, plaster on the biggest grin I can manage, then spin around. "Wells, my man! How've you been?"

He doesn't smile back. "You've come to see Bash, right?"

I inwardly groan. There's no way he's going to let me walk away now that he's spotted me. He'll do worse than Declan and Ryder. At least they tried their best not to hurt me. I'm not positive, but I'm pretty sure Wells would shoot me in the leg just to ensure I didn't get away.

"Of course," I state as I walk toward him.

He steps aside to let me go first, following so close behind it feels like he's afraid I'll bolt. I almost laugh, because honestly, he's not wrong. If I thought I could get away with it, I'd be halfway down the block by now.

The elevator ride up is torture. My heart won't slow down, and my cheeks ache from the fake smile I've been wearing like armor. It's been a long time since I've had to force it this hard, and every second it stays plastered on, I feel myself cracking underneath.

When the doors finally ding open on Bash's floor, my body locks up, refusing to move. Wells gives me a look, then basically shoves me forward, like I'm a kid about to face the principal. My stomach drops. There's no escape now.

Wells drapes an arm around my shoulders and steers me straight to Bash's door before I can second-guess myself. He knocks, firm and unbothered, while my stomach twists tighter and tighter. The second I hear movement on the other side, I squeeze my eyes shut. I can't do it. I can't see Bash's face yet. Not when I know his reaction might gut me.

I open them when Wells starts speaking. "Look who I found lurking outside the apartment."

Wells gives my shoulder a quick squeeze before letting go. My eyes find Bash, and the surprise on his face makes my chest tighten. He doesn't say a single word. He just steps forward and pulls me into a hug so tight it nearly knocks the air out of me. And then he holds on, like he has no intention of letting go.

I laugh and pat his back. "How's it going, bro?"

He pulls back and holds me at arm's length with his hands on my shoulders, looking me over. "How's it going? How do you think it's going? You've been gone for over a fucking month and no one could find you."

I cringe, shrug my shoulders and say, "Sorry."

"Get the fuck in here," Bash demands, yanking me inside while Wells closes the door.

I find Amelia just inside, staring at me. There are tears in her eyes as she gives me a hug.

"We've been so worried, Jake," she whispers in my ear.

Well, fuck. I clear my throat to stop the tightness in it. Pulling away, I grab her hands, about to say something, but I'm distracted by what I feel on her hand.

I pull it up to my face and ask excitedly, "Are you two engaged?!"

She gives a small smile and nods. I look at my brother, who still looks pissed at me, but happy.

"You'd know if you didn't disappear on us," he says, pulling me away from his fiancée and pushing me down the hall to his office.

I laugh. "Alright, I'm here. You can let go."

"You'll be lucky if I ever let you out of this apartment," he says seriously.

Ugh, I don't doubt the seriousness of that. I hope he can understand why I disappeared, and why I need a little more time. I'm not usually completely forthcoming with Bash, but I feel like I'm going to have to give a little now.

"Sit," he demands, and I obey. "Start talking."

"It's a long story…" I start, but he interrupts.

"I don't care if we sit here all night. You're going to tell me everything, and we're going to figure this out," he says.

"What did James tell you?" I ask.

He shakes his head. "Nothing. He said he found you and you were fine but wanted more time to figure things out. He didn't say what, or where, or how. I came really close to hurting my best friend, Jake, so you better have something good for me."

I shake my head and sigh. "I'm sorry. I wasn't in the best place after Everly's wedding and with Dad throwing me out. I just needed to escape for a while and figure out my life. I didn't have anything left to my name."

Bash's anger fades a little. "Dad's an asshole, but why didn't you come to me?"

I shrug.

"Why, Jake?"

"Because I was embarrassed, okay?" My anger comes out. "You've always been the better son. I'm a fuck-up. No matter how hard I tried to be good at my job and make Dad proud, I did the opposite."

"You're not a fuck-up, Jake." Bash has said this before, but it doesn't change how I feel.

I just shrug and lean back further in my chair.

"Jake… Dad is worried about you too. He has been searching. We all have."

"Why would he be worried? He doesn't want me to take over the business. I'm not even the son he wants," I say, looking away for a moment because I'm sick of seeing pity on his face.

My attention is drawn back to Bash as he laughs.

"What's so funny?" I ask, getting angrier.

"You realize Dad told me that he wanted you, not me, right? He's always had you in mind to take over his business."

"What?" I ask, genuinely shocked Dad would say that.

Bash nods. "He told me when he cut you off, he was doing it in hopes you'd take things more seriously. He didn't want you to continue partying and having random girls warm your bed. He wanted you to settle down."

This time I laugh. I really don't understand what my father's problem is, especially since his issue with me isn't even true. Well, part of it. I did party a good bit, but I was usually smart about it. I know Bash believes the same thing as my father, though.

"Now why are you laughing?" Bash asks.

"Nothing," I say, not wanting to get into it.

What's the point? I know Bash is my brother, but would he really believe me if I told him that the image he had of me wasn't completely true all along? If I do that, I'll have to explain why I let people believe that, and I'm not ready for that conversation yet. I probably never will be.

Bash shakes his head. "So, are you coming home or not, Jake?"

I shrug. "What's the point?"

Bash groans loudly and throws his hands up to his head, pulling at his hair. "Fucking hell, Jake. The point is that everyone misses you, and we want you home. Tell me what I can do to help."

My heart squeezes at his words. I know they miss me, but they don't even know the real me. They miss the fake me. I don't know if I'm ready to come home to that yet. Actually, I know I'm not. I still have to figure things out with Jules too, but I know in order to leave Bash's apartment, I have to give him something.

"Ah, you know I'm coming home. I just need a little more time, okay?"

Bash has on his concerned thinking face. If I were to guess, he was plotting ways he could tie me up and keep me here until I talked or came back.

"Dad's ready to give you everything back," he states.

Well, that's honestly a surprise. "Why the change of heart?"

Leaning forward, he says, "Like I said, he's worried about you, and to me that means he misses his son."

Well good for fucking him. Maybe he shouldn't have kicked me out in the first place. Then again, if he hadn't, I never would have met Jules. I would still be stuck in the same mundane fake life that I hate.

We're both silent for too long. Minutes go by, and I'd say it's getting awkward, but we're both lost in our thoughts.

"You don't want to come home, do you?" he asks with a frown.

My heart sinks, but I truly consider his words. Do I want to come home? I do, but not now. If I came home now, I'd fall right back into the same rut I've been in. I can't waste the past month.

I don't respond, so he continues. "Where are you staying, Jake? Do you have any money?"

I plaster the fake smile back on. "I'm staying with a friend, and yeah, I have money. I got a job with another buddy and am doing fine. Great, actually."

It's true. I hate to admit it, but this is the happiest I've been in a long time. Even though the management job sucks, it's not horrible. Tristan ensures I get nights and weekends off, plus I get to work with Jules every day. I may not have my own place, but I've never felt this free before.

I've always carried the thought that I was coming home, but it was never really for me. I told myself I'd come back for my friends, for Bash. I love them, and I'd miss them if I didn't, but does that mean I have to slip back into the life I left behind? Could I still see them, still be part of their world, while keeping the life I've built for myself? That thought... it feels kind of freeing.

I shake the thoughts away. This is not the time to think about all of it. I should have sorted through everything instead of just living my new life, pretending the old one didn't exist. That was easier, but deep down I knew the two worlds would eventually collide.

I don't know what Bash sees on my face, but he says, "Okay. Continue taking the time to figure out whatever you need to, but don't shut us out. Everly needs you, and honestly, so do the rest of us. Ben's probably been more of a mess than I have, so just send him a text or something, okay?"

"Yeah, okay. I'll text you too, so you have my new number."

Bash rounds his desk, and I stand as well. He pulls me in for another hug before saying, "Promise you won't disappear."

Wow, my emotions are getting the better of me. I clear my throat before replying. "I promise."

He pats me on the shoulder. "Alright, get out of here. Wells is going to take you wherever you need to go."

"I don't need Wells..." I start, but Bash interrupts.

"He's taking you," he says.

I laugh. "Alright, fine. I'll see you at the gender reveal."

He nods and walks me out the front door. Wells is already standing outside of it, somehow knowing that Bash would need him. They exchange a look, no words, before Wells leads me down to the car. I don't even think Stan and I were that good at being able to read each other's minds. Then again, I was never super close to the guy.

"Where to?" he asks.

I know Bash wants to know where I'm staying, but I don't want him to know that yet. Besides, I have a lot of thinking to do, and I know exactly where I do that best.

Chapter Twenty

Jules

My heart is pounding, and sweat is soaking through my shirt like I just ran a marathon. Who am I kidding? I don't run. I've never run. I used to have stamina for three-hour rehearsals, but that doesn't prepare you for that kind of torture. Why does anyone run willingly?

"Jules," Eric spits out, interrupting my thoughts.

Eric sits at the island while I stand on the other side, staring at him. My hands feel clammy, my stomach twists into knots, and I can't sit. Not with my heart hammering like this, not with every nerve in my body screaming at me. I need to tell him now. I have to. I can't put it off any longer.

"Yes?" I ask, knowing he only said my name to get my attention back on him.

He shakes his head. "Just tell me what's going on."

"I can never dance again," I spit out so fast that I barely understood what I just said.

His eyes widen and mouth hangs open. "Come again?"

I take a deep breath and let it out before I repeat in a low voice, and slower, "I can never dance again."

"What do you mean?" he asks calmly.

Closing my eyes, I will myself to keep calm. "I broke my knee and ankle. The same leg that the doctors told me to be careful on... I'll never be able to dance like before. I'll never be on Broadway."

Eric's eyebrows squeeze together with a lot of emotions crossing his face. This is exactly what I was afraid of. He's thinking that everything everyone sacrificed for my dreams was pointless.

"When did this happen?" he asks, peeking around the island like he's looking for my injured leg.

"A few months ago..."

"Are you kidding me?!" he shouts.

I cringe and don't respond.

He takes his glasses off, placing them on the counter as he rubs his eyes. Yeah, he's mad.

Sighing, he asks, "Why didn't you tell me?"

I shrug my shoulders.

"Jules... what have you been doing for work?" he asks, calming down.

"I'm working as a housekeeper at a hotel," I state, embarrassed.

"Seriously?" Eric asks, standing from the island, pacing.

"I'm sorry..." I say, knowing an apology isn't going to help anything.

"Jules..." He shakes his head. "I... Ugh, never mind. Do you have enough money for the apartment?"

"Yes, I turned it in before coming back. I'm making enough," I state.

He stares at me, and I have no idea what that look is. Is it pity or fury? Yeah, I figured he would be angry. I know my brother loves me and cares about me, but there was no way around him being mad that I can never dance again. All that money and time down the drain. I fucked up.

He rubs his hand through his hair. "Do Mom and Dad know?"

"No," I reply.

Shaking his head again, he walks toward the door.

"Where are you going?" I ask, my heart pounding harder now.

"I need some time to process this. I'll call you later," he says as he walks out the door, slamming it.

I stand there staring at the front door. Did he really just walk out? I feel a tear slipping down my cheek. Ugh. I knew he'd be pissed, but is this it? Is this where he no longer wants to be my brother? Did I fuck everything up? I can't help the laugh that escapes as I think about how he doesn't even know about Jake. This is it. I'm losing my brother, and maybe even my parents when they find out their daughter is worthless.

I pull out my phone and text Jake, praying that he's free.

Meet me at the rooftop?

Jake

Already there.

When I make it to the rooftop, he's lying on the ground, looking like he's asleep. The fact that he was already at the rooftop when I texted tells me that his talk with his brother didn't go well either.

"Hey," I say, lying down next to him.

"Hey," he responds in a low voice.

We spend the next hour staring up at the sky, letting the quiet stretch between us. I'm curled against him, his arm tucked under my neck, his warmth pressing into me. The steady rhythm of his breathing against my shoulder is grounding, and for once, I don't have to fight the chaos in my own head. It's comforting just to exist here with him, to not have to say a word, yet knowing he's right there if I need him, if I falter, if I break.

Jake breaks the silence. "If five years from now I was still poor, would you still be with me?"

I sit up to get a better look at him. "Of course I would."

He laughs and sits up facing me. "Really? If I stayed a hotel manager forever, you'd still be my girlfriend?"

I tap my finger to my chin like I'm thinking. "Well, I do have a problem with that." His face falls, so I quickly add, "I would hope I'd be your wife by then."

He stares at me for a moment, with that familiar spark in his eyes, before the smile returns. Then he leans in, pulling me into a kiss. I let him, softly at first, but eventually I push him back. As much as I know we both like the idea of escaping into each other, tonight feels different. Tonight, I think we really need to talk.

"How did it go with your brother?" I ask.

He shrugs. "As good as it could. It got me thinking about what I want for my future. I miss him and my friends, but I'm not sure I want to go back to that life."

I nod, trying to grasp what he's saying, but I'm not sure I can. I have no idea what his old life was like. I would give anything to go back to mine. It feels cruelly ironic. He can return to something he clearly doesn't want, while I'm trapped, unable to go back to something I desperately do.

Grabbing my hand and rubbing it, he asks, "What about you? How'd it go with Eric?"

I shrug my shoulder to pretend like what happened doesn't bother me before I speak, but my emotions betray me. Tears stream down my face, and he immediately pulls me in for a hug while I sob against him. Damn it. I thought I was fine, but clearly this past hour was just me hiding it. How come I can keep my emotions in check until someone asks me about it?

"Hey, it's okay. Tell me what happened," he says soothingly.

I sit back and wipe away my tears. "He walked out on me. I told him that I'll never be able to dance again, and he got mad and walked out, saying he'll call later."

Jake looks at me confused, then angry. "Why would he do that?"

I shrug my shoulders. "I assume because he's mad that it was all a waste."

Shaking his head, Jake says, "No. I can't imagine that's what it is. Maybe he was just mad that you kept it from him for so long."

"I don't know. It didn't seem like that's what it was. Whatever, it doesn't matter," I say, laying back down, looking at the sky, wishing we could see the stars.

Jake lies back with me, and we drift in silence for a long while. I almost think he's asleep until he shifts, pulling me in even closer. It's like he's wrestling with something in his head and needs the quiet comfort of holding me to get through it.

I love this. Being in Jake's arms makes everything else fade until it doesn't exist. I don't think about work, or family, or anything else that normally weighs on me. All that matters is him, and the way his body fits against mine. Every worry, every fear, every doubt feels distant and small. In this moment, it's just us, and I never want it to end. It's me and Jake against the world.

I decide to ask him a thought that pops into my head every now and then. "Do you ever think about running away? Just leaving it all and starting over?"

Jake laughs as he responds, "That's pretty much what I'm doing now, so yeah."

"No. I mean like, go to another state or even country. Completely disappear with no intention of ever coming back to your old life."

Jake takes longer to respond this time. "I've thought about it, but I know I can't. I'd miss my friends and family. Plus, I just couldn't do that to them."

I nod. He's right. Eric would go crazy if I just disappeared and was never heard from again. My parents would too. I know ultimately I would miss them, but that doesn't make the thought sound any less appealing.

Jake rolls on top of me and pushes the hair out of my face. "Is that what you're thinking? Do you want to disappear?"

I stare at him, not having an answer. I'd be lying if I said no.

"Does that mean you'd go without me?" he asks sadly.

My eyes widen. "Would you come with me?"

He kisses me on the forehead. "I'd go anywhere with you, Jules. I'm an all-in type of guy. If you leave, I'll follow."

"What about everyone else? Your friends and brother?" I ask.

He rolls off me and stares at the sky again, thinking for a moment. "I don't know, but all I know is that you're the only one I can't live without."

My heart squeezes. How can I respond to that? Does he really feel that way about me? We haven't known each other that long, but there's an undeniable connection between us. Maybe it's because we're both drowning, but is that really a good thing? If we're both sinking, who's going to save us? Will we stay under together, or will one of us find the courage to break the surface? And if they do, will they come back for the other, or leave them behind?

Groaning, I push those thoughts out of my head. It doesn't matter right now. What matters is that at this moment, Jake and I have each other and we're here. We're as happy as we can be, and we're surviving this life together.

Chapter Twenty-One

Jake

The past two weeks blur together, gone faster than I can hold onto them, and I'm more confused than ever. I've spent more nights tangled up in Jules' apartment than I have at Eric's. We've been losing ourselves in each other, drowning in every kiss, every touch. I know it can't last forever, but it feels too good to let go.

Right now, all I want is to be with Jules. I regret giving my phone number to my old friends and incorporating myself back into their lives. I messaged Ben, who was furious with me as well, and Everly. She was a lot more forgiving and looking forward to seeing me at the gender reveal, which is today. Everly and I have been texting daily, acting like nothing has changed between us.

Speaking of Everly, she texted me while I was getting ready.

Everly

I'm looking forward to seeing you to-day!

I text back a quick *me too* and leave it at that. I know she's only sending it to make sure I won't back out at the last minute, her way of reminding me she'd be upset if I didn't show. The thought makes my chest tighten, but I keep moving, and finish getting ready. In the mirror, I practice the only armor I have left... plastering on a smile that doesn't reach my eyes.

And that's the problem. I'm back to wasting all my energy pretending, lying through my teeth to the people I've known my whole life. Especially Everly. She's a therapist, trained to notice every flicker of expression, every change in tone. One wrong look and she'll see straight through me, and I can't let that happen. With her, I have to be on guard constantly, and it's exhausting. But with Jules, it's different. There's no mask, no pretending. I'm genuinely happy when I'm with her. And even when I'm not, she doesn't make me feel broken. She just stays.

After getting ready in the bathroom and talking myself into some kind of courage, I walk out to find Jules stretched across the couch. My heart kicks up, and before I can overthink it, I drop down beside her and pull her into a kiss. It's meant to be quick, but it lingers. It lasts longer than I intended, and by the time I pull back, my pulse is racing.

"Wow, you look handsome," she says, looking me over in appreciation.

I smirk. "Yeah? Want to distract me a little and keep me in bed all day?"

She laughs and pushes me off her. "Nope. Sorry, I'm not going to be the reason you break a promise to your friends."

I groan. She knows I'm supposed to be at a gender reveal party, but I really don't want to go. It's not Everly and James. I'm thrilled for them, and I want to celebrate this new chapter in their lives. That part is easy. What isn't easy is the thought of walking into a room filled with everyone from my old life. Smiling, hugging, pretending like I haven't been avoiding them. The idea of facing all of that feels suffocating.

Jules offered to come with me, but I decided it's better if she doesn't. It isn't that I don't want her to be there. I'm just not ready for my two worlds to collide. She still doesn't know much about who I really am, or who I was. I haven't told her that I am, or was, a billionaire. Part of me believes it wouldn't change how she sees me, but the other part is terrified to test it.

"It'll be fine, Jake. Go for a couple of hours and then come home. I'll be waiting for you," she says with a sexy smirk.

I groan again as I stand. "I'll be back in two hours."

She laughs. "No, take your time."

She walks me to the door, and I can't take my eyes off her. She's beautiful. Perfect, really. She didn't even take offense when I said I wanted to go to the party alone. Instead, she reassured me that she understood and that she'd love to meet my friends and family when I'm ready. How did I get so lucky to have her in my life? Now all I have to do is not screw it up.

She kisses me and pulls away. "Have fun, Jake. Your friends love you. You don't have to pretend."

I give her a small smile before walking out the door and thinking about what she just said. I've been honest with her about how I feel and why I'm having trouble going back to my old life. She's been so fucking understanding, and I don't know what I did to deserve her. She might be right, but today isn't the day to stop pretending. I won't screw up this important day for Everly.

Standing outside James and Everly's apartment feels strange. I've walked up to this door countless times before, but today the air feels heavier. I force myself to shake it off and psych up enough courage to knock. Before my hand makes contact, the door swings open, and Bash is there, his eyes narrowing in concern as he takes me in. My stomach twists, but I slap on that fake-ass smile like armor and brush past him with a quick, careless "hey."

He places his hand on my shoulder after closing the door and says, "I'm really glad you came, Jake."

I laugh. "You say that as if you thought I would break my promise."

He doesn't say anything as he stares at me with furrowed brows.

I'm not sure I want to know his response to that, and thankfully I don't have to find out as Ben comes up behind me and pins me against the wall.

"Geez, Ben," I groan, trying to push him off.

Ben ignores me, keeping his body close. This is odd.

"I'm not going to run away, man. I'm here. You can relax," I say, grinning.

Ben looks really pissed, and like he's going to tear my head off. I flinch as he leans in, but relax when he wraps me in the tightest hug he's ever given me. Damn.

"I'm still fucking pissed at you, Jake, but I'm glad you're here and alive," he whispers in my ear and then finally pulls away, giving me some breathing room.

I pat him on the shoulder and move away from the wall before he decides to throw a punch. Looking around the room, I find everyone staring at me. Everyone but James and Everly, who are probably still upstairs, getting ready.

I give a wave to the room and say, "Hey," but quickly return to my brother's side like he's my personal bodyguard against everyone.

Thankfully, the awkwardness doesn't last. Everly and James come down the stairs, and Everly is glowing. She's never looked happier. A fitted green dress hugs her frame, barely revealing her tiny baby bump. I thought she'd be bigger by now. She's radiant, with her brownish-red hair curled over her shoulders, and every bit as beautiful as I remember.

Her friends, Ashley and Paige, meet her at the bottom of the stairs as James comes to join us over in the corner of the room.

"I'm glad you made it, Jake," James says with a pat on my shoulder. Dang everyone's so touchy today.

Everly's small hazel eyes meet mine, and I plaster the grin wider on my face as I walk toward her. "Everly!"

After wrapping my arms around her in a hug, she says, "Jake, I've missed you. I'm glad you could make it."

My smile falters a little, feeling guilty. I shake the thoughts out of my head, knowing that I'm here now and that's all that matters. I can't imagine if I had missed such a big day in her life. Would she have forgiven me? Would I have forgiven myself?

Bash interrupts my thoughts and goes in for a hug with Everly next. "Beautiful as always, Everly."

I step aside while everyone else greets her, my eyes scanning the room for Declan. He's nowhere in sight. Everly told me during one of our daily texts that he's the one that knows the gender and is handling the reveal plans. I teased her about letting me take that role instead, but she shot me down instantly, with no hesitation.

Everly's father lets her know that Declan just pulled up with the cake and would be up shortly.

I step up beside her and joke, "I still can't believe you didn't trust me with the surprise."

She laughs. "Jake, how can you not believe that? You would totally use this as a prank. I can see it now. You would have told us the opposite gender just to completely mess with us and see our reaction when the baby is born."

I gasp and place my hand over my heart, feigning to be hurt. "I would never!"

Everyone laughs because they know it's true. Even if I didn't mess with them, they would've questioned it the whole time, which would've been a prank in itself. I do miss this. I miss the fun we all had together… the pranks, the laughter. Maybe coming back to all this won't be as bad as I've been imagining. Especially if Jules is by my side.

Declan enters, carrying a large cake box. While everyone's attention is on him, I take my phone out to text Jules.

> I miss you. I wish I would've brought you.

Her text comes back immediately, as if she's been waiting for me to text her.

Jules

> Is everything going okay? I miss you too.

> It is. I just wish you were here.

Jules

> Next time. Enjoy the time with your friends.

I know I'm smiling at my phone as Bash bumps me with his shoulder. "Why didn't you bring her?"

I look up at him questioningly. "What?"

"You obviously have a girl. Why not bring her?"

I shrug my shoulders. "I didn't think it was the right time. How did you know I met someone?"

Bash laughs. "When we talked a couple of weeks ago, I could see it on your face. She's the reason you weren't ready to come home. Does she know who you really are?"

I glance away, teeth sinking into my bottom lip. I know exactly what he's asking, but the truth twists inside me. Because in a way, she does. She knows the real me, the broken me, the one weighed down by demons I can barely name. Not the billionaire part, not the life I left behind, but the parts I hide from everyone else.

Still, I give him the answer he's waiting for. "Not yet."

He nods, and our attention is pulled back to what's happening at the party. Declan is refusing to let Everly cut the cake, so she's arguing with him. The smile that spread across my face isn't forced or fake. I've missed this.

We all gather around the island, waiting in anticipation for the big reveal. James cuts the cake while Everly's hand is on top of his. They lift the knife, remove the slice and place it on a plate behind the cake, where only they can see it.

Their faces light up, and they yell out in unison, "It's a girl!"

We all cheer and clang our glasses of champagne together, congratulating them.

Ben steps up and asks, "What's her name going to be?"

"Lauren," Everly states.

That's perfect. My throat tightens with emotion, and I look around the room to find everyone else doing the same. Ashley has tears in her eyes, but she's happy. Lauren was Ashley and Everly's best friend in high school, who took her own life because she didn't see a future worth living.

I didn't spend a lot of time with her, but I noticed. I noticed her fake smiles, her depression, and how hopeless she looked. When I was around, I tried to do everything I could to make her smile and laugh, but it wasn't enough. I knew it wasn't. Ben took it the hardest, other than obviously those closest to her. I was the only one who knew the depths Lauren's death affected him. He really cared for her and blamed himself for not doing more. There was nothing he could've done, but that doesn't ease the pain and guilt.

I'm blindsided by a memory of Lauren back in high school.

Lauren slips into class and drops into the seat in front of me. Her shoulders slump, her hair hiding most of her face, and even from behind I can tell something's off. She's been carrying that cloud around for weeks, but today it looks heavier. I hate it.

She came here in the middle of the school year, all shy, scared, and sad. We don't talk much, but I always try to make her laugh with the dumb things I do and say in class. She doesn't deserve to walk around like she's dragging the world behind her. She looks different now, and it's not just the new haircut or dyed-black hair. Lauren's supposed to be laughing at my jokes and rolling her eyes at me when I'm annoying, not whatever this is.

I drum my pencil against the desk, waiting for the right moment. She doesn't react. Not even a flinch. Okay, desperate times.

I lean forward, close enough so only she can hear me. "So, you know Ben, right? Did you know he screams when he sees a squirrel?"

Nothing. Not even a twitch.

"Yeah," I go on, "claims they're 'shifty-eyed rodents plotting against him.' Last week one ran across him while he was sitting against a tree. He screamed like a little girl."

Her shoulders jerk. She's fighting a smile.

"And get this," I whisper. "He swears he saw one wink at him once. An actual wink. He says it was their leader, probably marking him as a target. Now he won't eat lunch outside."

Her hand goes up to cover her mouth, and I see it, the little shake of her shoulders.

I lean in even closer, dropping my voice. "Don't tell him I told you, but he carries sunflower seeds in his backpack. Calls it 'squirrel insurance,' just in case they try to take him out."

She glances at Ben's backpack, where a bag of sunflower seeds sits in the mesh side pocket. That does it. She bursts out laughing, loud and unstoppable. The whole class turns, and I grin like I've just pulled off a miracle.

"See?" I say, laughing with her.

Mr. Henderson narrows his eyes. "Something you two would like to share with the class?"

I lean back in my chair, dead serious. "Yeah. That Ben is currently in a turf war with squirrels, and I don't think he's winning."

Ben stares at me with a what-the-fuck look on his face while Lauren laughs harder.

Mr. Henderson slams his book shut, glaring like I've ruined his life. "Detention, Jake."

Totally worth it. Lauren is still laughing, and that's all I care about.

Laughter pulls me out of the memory. While everyone's distracted, I slip into another room for a moment of privacy. It's frustrating how easily things like this can trigger me. I'd been doing so well, and now the weight of it all drags me down again. Leaning against the wall, I take a slow breath and try to find my way back to the mindset I had before, focusing on the happiness of this moment.

I'm glad it's a girl, and they are naming her Lauren. I won two bets with Everly a while back, so I'm lucky enough to choose her nickname and the color of the nursery. I know exactly what they'll be. Ben and I had a nickname for Lauren that only the three of us knew about, so we'll use that. And Lauren's favorite color will be the nursery color. I know Everly probably thinks I'll come up with something crazy, but I can't think of anything more perfect than honoring her like that.

I didn't notice anyone come in until I felt a hand on my shoulder.

"You doing okay?" Asher asks, looking down at me.

I fake another smile and say, "Yeah, just needed a break from the chaos. I haven't been around this many people in a while."

Thankfully, that's not a lie because freaking Asher is impossible to lie to.

"It means a lot to Everly to have you here, Jake. She loves you," he says, backing up a little.

"Yeah, I know."

"If you need anything..." Asher starts, but I interrupt him.

"I know Asher. Thanks."

He nods and walks off, leaving me to collect myself. I take another deep breath and step back into the room. I linger only a few more minutes before saying my goodbyes, and of course, everyone makes sure I know I better not run away again. Their teasing warnings earn a small, guilty smile from me, but I can feel the tension in my chest easing just a little.

After exiting the building, I see another familiar face I haven't seen in a while. Once again, the smile on my face is genuine as I walk toward Stan and wrap him in a hug. I debate giving him that big, fat kiss on the cheek I promised myself I would. Seeing him in person again, I decide that's going a little too far. I study him for a moment, noticing how much he's aged in just a few months, the deeper lines carved around his tired brown eyes, and the weight that sits heavy on his face. His dark brown hair is cut in a sharp military style. He still looks good for a man in his fifties.

"What are you doing here?" I ask as I pull away.

He pats me on the back. "I needed to see with my own eyes that you were alive."

Laughing, I say, "Well here I am."

Stan turns serious and shakes his head. "Why'd you disappear?"

Shrugging, I respond, "I just needed some time away from everything."

"I would've helped you stay hidden, you know..." Stan says, trailing off.

That makes me emotional again. Would he really have? Stan has been with me for what feels like forever, but would he have kept my whereabouts from my friends and family? Especially since he's still on my father's payroll?

"I wouldn't have told anyone," he says, reading my mind.

"Fuck Stan. I'm sorry."

"It's okay. Are you coming home?" he asks.

"Not yet."

"You have my number when you're ready, and you need me," he says, walking back toward his car.

"Hey Stan," I yell, and he stops, looking back.

"Yeah?"

"Thank you... for everything," I say, meaning it. He has no idea how much I've come to appreciate what he's done for me.

He nods before heading back to his car, and I stand there, watching until he drives out of sight. On the walk back to Jules' apartment, my mind spins with a question I can't shake... how do I blend who I've become with the person I used to be?

Chapter Twenty-Two

JULES

"You're cheating," I pout.

Jake laughs. "How am I cheating?"

I growl as my ball misses the hole again. "I don't know, but you are."

Jake continues laughing as he watches me get angry at the stupid ball, which won't go in the stupid hole. I hate mini golf. I don't know how I let him talk me into playing.

"You're not very good at this, are you?" he asks, holding back a smile.

"Shut up," I say as I finally give up, pick up the ball, and slam it into the hole. Of course, it pops right back out. "Are you kidding me?!"

This time, Jake bursts into a full-on belly laugh, dropping onto the nearby bench to keep from toppling over. I glare at him, but it's impossible to stay mad. His laughter is contagious, and before I know it, my anger melts away. I slide onto the bench beside him, and we're both laughing, the tension between us dissolving with every breath.

"I've never seen this side of you before," he says as his laughter subsides.

"Oh yeah? What? Anger? You've seen that before," I say, remembering how a while back I basically threw that fit at work.

"No, competitive. I think I like it," he says, leaning over to kiss me.

I push him off before his lips meet mine. "Nope, I'm not going to fall for it. You're cheating, and I'm going to find out how."

He stands up and continues to laugh as we walk toward the next hole. I am really competitive and can get angry easily when losing, but with Jake, he eases the anger. As we reach the next hole, my phone buzzes with a text. I take it out to read.

Bro

Jules, I said I was sorry. Please call me or let's meet for dinner. We need to talk about this.

I groan and swipe out of the texts with my brother, going back to the main text screen. Jake was looking over my shoulder, reading my text. I turn off my phone and place it back in my pocket, ignoring it.

"You should really talk to him, Jules," Jake says with concern in his eyes.

I shrug. "I'm not in the mood."

"He misses you."

I roll my eyes. "Yeah, well, maybe he shouldn't have walked out angrily the day I was willing to talk to him."

Jake shakes his head. "He just needed time to process…"

I interrupt him. "Are you really going to defend him?"

Jake holds up his hands in defense. "No. I'm on your side. I just think you should talk to him to clear the air. He's your brother."

I sigh. I know he's right. "I'm not ready yet."

Jake nods and changes the subject. "So, Onion?"

I laugh. "Were you looking at my texts over my shoulder?"

He grins. "Maybe."

I shrug. "I told you that was your nickname. You remember that night, right?"

"I remember it. How could I forget?" he asks.

"Have a problem with Onion?" I ask.

"Nope. I was just hoping that maybe you would've changed my name to boyfriend, or daddy or something," he states seriously.

This time I laugh. "Daddy? Gross. Don't tell me that's one of your kinks."

His eyes narrow, and he steps closer. "You can call me whatever you like in bed."

"Alright, Onion it is."

He shakes his head and hits the ball straight into the hole. Damn it.

"Let's finish up here and head back, shall we?"

Instead of heading straight back to the apartment, we stop at a restaurant for lunch. It's busy, so we take a seat at the bar. Honestly, a glass of wine doesn't sound so bad right now. After placing our orders, a man sits down in the empty seat beside me. Jake looks over and glares at him. I try to hide the smile spreading on my lips. I like when he's territorial over me.

"It's a beautiful afternoon, isn't it?" the man asks, looking at me.

He is handsome. He has a hat on, but his blonde hair sticks out of it. His piercing green eyes don't leave mine, waiting for a response. I just nod.

"Hank," he reaches out his hand for me to shake, but his eyes are on Jake.

I look at Jake and back at the stranger's hand. "Um..."

Jake leans over me to say something to him. "What are you doing here, Hank?"

Hank grins and takes a sip of his beer, which I didn't notice before. "I thought it was time I met your girl."

Jake shakes his head and sighs.

"Do you know him?" I ask Jake, and he nods.

"Yeah, he's a good buddy. He found me quickly after I disappeared," he says, like he was annoyed with that fact.

I finally smile and hold my hand out to him. "Well, Hank, I'm Jules. Nice to meet you."

He shakes my hand, and I think Jake finally snaps because he stands up quickly and grabs Hank's arm, pulling him off his seat and toward the back by the bathrooms. Alright then...

Minutes later, they both come back, and Jake looks a little more relaxed, but not exactly happy Hank has intruded on our time together.

I've had some time to think about what Hank said while they were gone. "So, how did you know that we were here? You mentioned that it was time to finally meet me."

Hank smirks and looks toward Jake. "She's a smart one."

I lean my head to block Hank's view of Jake. "And I'm sitting right here in front of you."

There's nothing that annoys me more than being talked about like I'm not in the room or, heck, sitting right beside someone.

"Yes, you are. I have my ways to find people," he states ominously.

Well, that's... concerning. I don't ask him to elaborate because I have a feeling he won't. I wonder if he and Jake share their locations and maybe Jake mentioned he was hanging out with me today. I hope so at least.

"So, Jules, tell me how you ended up with someone like my buddy Jake here."

"How does anyone not end up with someone like Jake?" I challenge.

Hank keeps the grin on his face as he lifts his beer up in salute, like he's saying touché. I glance back at Jake, who is smiling. I was worried maybe Hank wasn't actually a friend of Jake's, but I can see that I'm wrong. He seems like a nice enough guy, just maybe someone who is rarely out in social situations and very blunt.

"So, you met Jake at work. You're a housekeeper, right?" he asks, and it's not judgy at all.

"I am," I state embarrassed, even though I know I shouldn't be.

"But you don't want to be," he states.

My eyes snap to his. Dang, he is perceptive.

I chuckle. "I don't know anyone who wants to clean up after people for the rest of their lives."

He shrugs. "Some people do enjoy it. If that's not what you want to do, then what is?"

I think about how to answer him for a moment. I don't need to go into detail about how my dreams will never come true. I decide to tell him what my ultimate goal has been since I was younger.

"I want to open a dance studio where cost doesn't hold any-one back. There are so many kids with the talent to be extra-ordinary, but they'll never get the chance because no one gave them a place to start."

Hank looks impressed, and Jake stares at me, shocked. I suppose I never told him that before. It's not really something I've thought about since my career ended. I've felt that everything in my life was taken away from me that day, but maybe I was wrong. Maybe I can still work toward my dream of opening a studio. It'll take a lot longer, and there will be more work because of the money it'll cost, but I could still do it. I could.

The longer I spend talking to Hank, the more I like the guy. I was right. He's blunt. He says pretty much whatever is on his mind, and he doesn't care if someone's going to take offense to it or not. They were joking around a bit too, which I enjoyed watching. I haven't seen Jake with any of his old friends, so meeting Hank was a nice surprise. I hope that Jake will let me meet his brother soon and maybe some of his other friends.

Jake gets up to use the bathroom, and Hank watches until he goes through the door.

"Finally," he says, blowing out a breath and looking back toward me. "How's he doing? Really doing?"

My heart races at his question, but I answer as truthfully as I can. "He's doing good. He's still struggling with some things, but he's getting there."

Hank nods. "Give me your number. I'm going to text you mine. If anything changes, call me. Or if you need anything, anything at all, call."

I'm a little stunned, but I give him my number anyway, right before Jake gets back and takes the seat next to me again.

I feel my phone buzz in my pocket, which I assume is Hank texting me his number. Right after that, he stands and says he has to go, but it was nice meeting me. I nod and watch him walk away, feeling like there is a lot more to that man than meets the eye.

"Well, that was a surprise," Jake says.

"It was nice meeting him. He's a good friend?" I ask, even though I already know the answer.

Jake nods. "Yeah, he is. He gets on my nerves, but he's one of the best guys I know. He'd do anything for his friends."

I can see that. He genuinely wanted to know how Jake is doing, which shows he understands the side of Jake he keeps hidden from everyone else. I can feel how much he cares, and I won't lie, I feel a pang of jealousy that I don't have someone like that in my own life.

"What's wrong?" he asks.

Ugh. As much as Jake makes it look easy to hide emotions, my facial expressions fail at that. "Nothing. I was just thinking that he seems to really care about you and that must be nice to have."

Jake looks at me seriously as he says, "I really care about you, Jules. Your brother does too."

Instead of letting his words sink in like I should, I ignore them, lean in, and kiss him. I'm not in the mood to deal with all this right now. I'm ready to head back and spend the night in Jake's arms. My boyfriend. My best friend. My everything.

CHAPTER TWENTY-THREE

JAKE

I finish straightening the tie on my suit and stare at myself in the mirror. I dress up for work every day, but this is different. This is fancier, and I know that where I'm going, everyone will be judging me. Not that I care... I just... I don't know anymore. I see my reflection in the mirror, but it's not me. It's not who I am anymore, and that scares me.

I've always hated these types of events, but I hate them even more now. The fake smiles, kissing ass, and the pretending to be better than everyone else when you know you're not. This is the stuff that I wouldn't miss if I left my past behind. I could still do it. I could do it with Jules. I don't have to attend these things or go back to my old life completely. I could stay where I'm at and live with Jules in her apartment. We'd be happy. That's what I've been considering a lot lately, but what she said last week made me reconsider that.

When Hank ambushed us at lunch, he got her to spill her dream in five minutes, something I hadn't managed in the months I've known her. Something I hadn't even considered asking her about. What kind of boyfriend am I?

So, the reason I'm doing this is for her. If she wants to open an affordable dance studio, she's going to need money. A lot of money. Money that past me used to have and present me doesn't.

My brother invited me to his charity event at work, and I accepted, knowing I need to get back in the game. I wanted to bring Jules with me, but I'm scared. Scared of failing, of letting her down. Scared that I'll realize I'm no longer cut out for this world and that I won't be able to give her the support she needs to chase her dreams. She's already endured the heartbreak of losing her dance career. I couldn't stand to be the cause of more pain.

A knock on my door pulls me out of my thoughts. "Shouldn't we leave Jake?"

I take a deep breath and let it out with one more glance in the mirror to make sure I look perfect. I do.

I open the door to find Eric on the other side, looking better than I've ever seen him before. I whistle. "Look at you, Eric."

He laughs. "Yeah, same to you. This is the Jake I know."

We're both silent as we inspect each other. The world we're heading into is so different from the one we're both currently living in.

"Alright, let's go. Stan should be waiting outside," I say as we walk out the front door together.

"Thanks again for inviting me. I appreciate it."

"Of course. It'll be good for you," I reply.

I invited Eric because this will be a great opportunity for him to network. I owe this to him. We both know that I could ask my brother to give Eric a job at his company, but Eric wouldn't accept that. He wants to earn his way to wherever he's headed, and honestly, he's going to great places. He's smart, charming, and loyal.

"I would've thought you'd have brought your girlfriend with you," he states.

Yeah, he's been trying to get out of me that I'm seeing someone. It's obvious, since I'm barely at his place anymore, that I'm staying over at hers. I hate lying to him. I want to tell him that I'm dating his sister, but I can't. They haven't patched things up yet.

"Nah, we're not that serious." The words taste bitter on my tongue.

Eric laughs. "I don't know. I've never known you to stick with the same girl for this long before. When do I get to meet her?"

My heart stops at his question, and my stomach twists. I want to tell him that he already knows her, but I can't. Yeah, that would go over well. *It's your sister, and I've been secretly fucking her behind your back.* Great. That would go perfectly.

I settle on the easiest answer. "Soon."

Stan drives us to the hotel where Bash's charity event is taking place. I have to admit, it's nice being driven around again. If I'm throwing myself back into this life, I might as well take the perks that come with it.

The moment we enter, Eric looks like he's going to be sick. "Man, this is really intimidating, isn't it?"

I laugh. "It is."

"How did you do this all the time?" he asks.

I lean in closer and whisper, "Lots of booze."

That gets a laugh out of him, but the laughter dies as he's staring at something... no, someone in the corner.

Shit. I didn't even think about her being here. "I'm sorry. I didn't think about who would be attending."

He shrugs, but I can tell he's affected. Yeah, I'm going to need to get him over to the bar as quickly as possible.

"Let's go," I say, leading him to the bar.

Unfortunately, we're caught before we're halfway there.

"Jake!" Everly yells my name, and we both freeze.

After turning around, her eyes widen as she takes in who I brought with me.

"Eric..." she whispers, and James protectively wraps his arm around her waist, sliding in beside her.

"Hi," Eric says, and I know that I need to interrupt before this gets too awkward.

"I brought Eric with me to network a bit. I thought it would help his career," I state.

Everly's smile brightens as she says, "That was a great idea, Jake. How are you doing, Eric?"

"Good," he says as he stares down toward her stomach, and back up.

Everly laughs. "Yeah, I'm not quite showing yet."

"Congratulations on the marriage... and baby," he struggles to get out.

"Thanks," James responds and whispers something to Everly.

She nods and says, "It was great seeing you. I hope you have a good time."

We watch them walk away, and we both let out a breath at the same time. I place my arm on his shoulder and continue leading him to the bar where we ask for the strongest drink to get us through the night.

"Well, that was..." Eric starts.

"Awkward," I finish, chugging my drink.

He laughs. "Yeah, that... So, you've seen her recently?"

I nod. "Yeah, I went to her gender reveal."

"How was that?"

I shrug. "Good. She's really happy. That's all I ever wanted for her."

"Me too... You're over her, aren't you?" he asks.

I think about it for a moment before responding. He's right. I am over her, and I'm not sure when it happened. Did it happen before she married James? Did it happen after the wedding? Or did it happen when Jules came into my life? Either way, I'm thankful. I loved Everly for so long and I still do, but it's not the same way that I love Jules. I don't think I ever actually felt the way I do about Jules for Everly.

Shit, did I just say I love Jules? I chug the rest of my drink, slamming it on the bar. Yeah, I guess I do. I fucking love Jules.

"I'm over her. I'll always love her, but not like that," I say.

"I want to ask how you got over her, but I can see the answer on your face," he says.

"What is that?" I ask.

"You love her, this girl you've been seeing," he states.

I don't answer, only smile, and that's all the response he needs. Well, that's enough about all this. I hate lying to Eric about his sister. I fucking love his sister, and I can't even tell him that. Eric and I have become good friends. I feel like shit betraying him like this, but it's not my choice. It's Jules' choice.

"Alright man, go walk around and network or find a pretty girl to take home tonight. Either way, it'll be a win," I say, pushing him away from the bar and walking in the opposite direction.

I intended to stay close to his side to help him through this, but I can't stand next to him when I'm lying to him. Plus, he'll probably be better off without me and my reputation around.

"So glad you made it, Jake." My brother walks up beside me with his beautiful fiancée by his side.

Amelia's wearing a dark blue dress that complements her pale skin. She's beautiful, but she definitely doesn't see it or carry herself with confidence. She's shy and would prefer to blend in. Too bad her red hair and blue eyes will never allow that.

I lean in to hug her. "You look beautiful, Amelia."

I know she's blushing as she pulls back. "You look handsome yourself. Happy to be back at these events?"

I want to laugh. Everyone thinks this is my scene, but they couldn't be more wrong. Honestly, I never really knew what my scene was until I met Jules. Quiet nights in with her... the girl I love. There it is again, that word. Yeah, that's my scene.

I shrug my shoulders and answer with the only truth I can muster. "It's been a while."

"I see you came with Eric," Bash interrupts, staring at him across the room.

"Yeah, I thought he could do some networking here," I respond.

"I didn't know you two were friends," he states.

I nod. "He has been letting me crash at his place."

Bash looks surprised. "How'd that happen?"

"I ran into him after the wedding. Told him I had nowhere to go, and he offered his spare room. I accepted, and we've become friends."

Bash and Amelia keep their eyes on Eric as they watch him talk to a woman. She looks like a supermodel. Tall, thin, tan skin. Her dark brown hair is up in a perfect bun. She looks familiar.

"Who's that?" I ask because clearly, they both know her.

Amelia grins. "That's my friend, Sierra. Don't you know her from Bash's office?"

I squint at her, trying to place her, and it makes sense why she's familiar. Then it clicks. "Oh yeah! It's been a while since I've seen her. She hired you as her assistant, right?"

Amelia nods. "Yep."

"And then you banged the boss. Way to use your friends to move up," I say jokingly.

Amelia laughs, but Bash glares at me.

"Alright, we need to make our rounds. Have fun, but stay out of trouble, Jake."

I salute Bash and watch him walk off as I order another drink. I glance at Eric from across the room, and it looks like he's really hitting it off with Sierra. Good for him. I decide to leave them be and mingle with the rest of the guests until it's socially acceptable to sneak out. I used to rely on hooking up with girls as my excuse to vanish, but I can't do that now. Not that I ever actually took anyone home. I just let everyone assume I did. Now, I actually have to be present and personable. But first, another drink.

Chapter Twenty-Four

JULES

J ake has been staying at Eric's place for the past couple of nights, and I'm not sure why. He said that he wanted to spend some time with my brother, and they went to an event together to help him network. It sounds legit, but I'm getting nervous thinking he's avoiding me. We've barely texted either.

I take a deep breath and pull out my phone. I'll be seeing him soon at work, but I need to know what I'm walking into.

I've missed you.

BF Onion

Missed you too. Get to work early?

My heart begins to race. Why does he want me to get to work early? Does he want to break up with me? Is that why he's been avoiding me? I just changed his freaking name in my phone to add BF for boyfriend in front of Onion.

Why?

I watch the dots appear, disappear, and reappear a couple of times before his response finally comes through.

BF Onion

So I can have some time with you in my office before work *winking emoji*

I let out a sigh of relief and smile as I read his message again. Okay, good. He doesn't want to break up with me or anything. That was a stupid thought. I don't know why I even considered that as an option.

Heading out now.

The moment I reach the hotel, Jake is already waiting outside the doors. Before I can even catch my breath, he's grabs my hand and pulls me through the lobby, up the elevator, and straight to his office. I haven't spent much time here since he finally got the space organized. It's small, nothing fancy, but just enough for him to handle what he needs, with a desk in the middle of the room, a computer on top, and a chair tucked neatly beneath it. Somehow, even in its simplicity, it feels intimate, like stepping into a corner of his world that's just for him and now, for me too.

He barely closes the door behind us before pressing me against the wall, his lips crashing onto mine.

"I've missed you so much, Jules," he murmurs between kisses, and my chest tightens at the sound of my name on his lips.

I laugh against his mouth. "It hasn't been that long…"

He pulls back slightly, trailing kisses down my neck, his voice low and teasing. "It hasn't been that long? Didn't you miss me?"

Every nerve in my body is on fire as he presses closer. My stomach twists, heat pooling where his touch lands. I try to focus, but it's impossible… every movement, every brush of his hand, sends shivers through me. His hand finds its way down the front of my pants and to my already damp underwear. That's embarrassing.

A cocky smirk tugs at his lips. "Mmm. I think your body missed me."

I can barely form words, only a breathy sound escaping me as he continues his relentless assault. My mind spins, caught between wanting more and the pull of anticipation.

"I've been trying to be good and keep business and pleasure separate, but… I need to fuck you against my desk. Do you want that?"

"Yes!" I say a little too enthusiastically.

He chuckles. "Take off your pants and panties."

I do as he says, and he undoes his buckle, but stops there watching me remove everything from my waist down.

He pulls me in for another bruising kiss and grabs my waist, guiding me to his desk. The world narrows until it's just the two of us, the air thick with electricity.

"Turn around and put your hands on the desk," he commands.

I hesitate, my heart pounding, and he steps closer, brushing against me, making it impossible to think. Apparently, I take too long, because he spins me, and I lose my balance, slamming my hands against the desk to hold myself steady. Without wasting any time, he spreads my legs apart with his foot, and I hear his zipper and shortly after the clang of his belt against the floor as his pants fall.

The moment stretches, heavy and charged, and I can feel him closer than ever with the heat radiating from him. My whole body is on alert, anticipating what's coming. I feel him pressing near, teasing, holding back just enough to make my mind spin. Without warning, he thrusts in.

"Fuck! Jules, you feel so good," he groans out as he kisses the back of my neck and presses my body harder against the desk.

I've never been fucked so relentlessly before, but I like it. A lot. Jake taking what he wants from me without apology is so hot. He's only about ten thrusts in, and I'm already about to explode.

"Jake…" I moan, the tension building.

"Fuck Jules. Say that again."

"Jake... Fuck me harder. Take everything from me," I say, chasing my own climax, needing more.

Jake groans and thrusts harder and faster than he ever has before, and it feels amazing. It doesn't take long before I'm riding my high and he quickly follows.

He pulls out of me and puts himself back together before grabbing my pants and underwear from the floor.

I grab them and look around his desk for a tissue. I'm about to reach for one when he says, "Don't."

"What?" I ask, confused.

He leans forward and growls in my ear. "I want my cum soaking your underwear all day so you're reminded of me while working."

I gasp and look him in the eye. I don't know what has gotten into him today, but this possessiveness... It's fucking hot.

I don't even bother putting my underwear back on yet as I kiss him fiercely. He lifts me up to sit on his desk and devours me like we haven't already had each other today, never mind just minutes ago.

He pulls away and groans. "Jules... if we don't stop, I'm going to take you again."

I giggle. "I wouldn't be opposed."

Shaking his head, he says, "I have a meeting in five minutes."

Sticking out my lip to make a pouty face, I ask, "Are you sure you can't be a little late?"

He stares at me for a moment before kissing me again and then places his forehead on mine. "Jules... I... I love you."

I freeze, and so does my heart. What? Did he really just tell me he loves me? Holy shit. I've never had anyone tell me they love me before.

Apparently, I take too long to respond because he's pulling away, looking hurt.

I yank him back quickly and kiss him just as hard as the first time. "I love you too, Jake."

His face lights up with the most gorgeous smile I've ever seen. This man is going to be the death of me.

He kisses me again, and then finally backs away so he's not touching me. "I really do have to go, but tonight, I'm going to make love to you all night, Jules."

I grin. "Maybe we can throw in a little fucking like this too?"

He laughs. "You like that? I'm sorry I just took you like that, but I couldn't wait a second longer. I fucking missed you."

Shaking my head, I respond, "I missed you too, and that was the best I've ever had."

Our smiles quickly fade when there's a knock on the door. I pull my underwear and pants on while Jake asks, "Yeah?"

"Mr. Hale, I have someone at the front desk asking to see you," the lady on the other side of the door says.

"Okay, you can bring them to my office. I'm almost done."

She leaves without a word, and I finish getting myself put back together. My hair is a mess, but I'll go fix that in the bathroom and put it up before starting work. Jake kisses me one more time before another knock is at the door. That was fast.

"I'll see you for lunch later," he says, opening the door.

I'm about to walk out when my foot freezes mid-step. The moment hits me like a punch to the chest because of who is on the other side of the door. Eric.

"Jules?" Eric asks, surprised.

We're all silent for a moment before Jake steps up beside me and opens the door wider. "Hey Eric, what's up?"

How he looks so calm I have no idea because on the inside I'm freaking out. Not only have I been ignoring my brother's phone calls, but he had no idea that I was working here with Jake. And Jake just literally fucked me against his desk a few minutes ago. Shit.

Chapter Twenty-Five

JAKE

Eric stands in the doorway, looking between me and Jules. I know he's trying to figure out what's going on between us because it's so obvious we just fucked with the way her hair is messed up. I watch Eric's face turn from confusion to anger in the blink of an eye.

"What's going on?" Eric's trying to hide his anger until he gets an answer.

"Eric... This is where I've been working..." Jules says nervously.

I'm just as nervous as she is, if not more, but I'm not going to show it.

"Why are you in his office?" Eric asks.

Jules' brows furrow as she looks at me and back to Eric. Jesus, Jules. You can't look any more suspicious if you tried.

Eric's anger is back and directed at me. "Are you screwing my sister?"

I keep a straight face, but don't answer. That must be answer enough because a fist flies at my face, hitting me directly in the jaw. I could've dodged him, but I deserved it. I've been fucking his sister behind his back when he told me she was off-limits. It's the only thing he's asked of me. He gave me a place to stay when I needed it. And friendship.

"Eric!" Jules yells while pushing him back.

"I don't know what to say." Eric's head hangs low while he shakes it.

"I'm sorry," I say sincerely.

"I want you out of my place by tonight," he responds.

Without another word, he walks out. Jules looks at me to see if I'm okay, but I give her a look that it's okay to follow him. She does, and it doesn't take long for her to catch up with him. I don't follow, but I can hear everything they're saying.

"Eric!" Jules yells.

"I'm not in the mood to talk, Juliet," he says, and I cringe at his tone.

"You have no right to tell me who I can and can't see," she responds with anger.

"You think that's what this is about? You can fuck whoever you want, Jules. Hell, I probably would have been happy to hear you and Jake were together, but that's the problem. I didn't hear about it. You've been lying to me about everything. About your injuries, your job, who you're seeing... I don't even know you anymore, Jules, and it sounds like you don't want me to. Point taken. Have a good life," he says, storming off, the stairwell door banging shut behind him.

I walk toward Jules, pulling her into a hug. "Hey, it's going to be alright. He just needs time to calm down and process everything."

Jules is sobbing in my arms, shaking her head. "No, it's not. He's right. I've kept everything from him, and I don't even know why..."

I hold her tighter and give her a few moments to let it all out. Once the crying stops, I step away for just a minute to cancel my meeting and everything else for the day. When I come back, she's gone. My heart races, and I pull out my phone to call her, noticing a text from Eric that I missed.

Eric

> I just had an interview with your brother's company and I'm about to be in the area. Mind if I stop by? It went great!

My heart sinks as I read his message. Eric was so fucking excited about it and he came to me first. He wanted to share his news with me as his friend, and I just fucked up everything. I feel like shit.

Pushing those thoughts to the side, I try calling Jules, who doesn't answer. I head to the front desk to be told she left feeling ill and won't be back today. I debate my next move. Do I head to her place to make sure she's okay, or do I go to Eric's and get my stuff out first? I decide if Jules isn't answering her phone, then she probably wants to be alone. I'll grab my stuff and see if she answers after. If not, then I'll grab a hotel room for the night and give her some space.

It doesn't take long to get my belongings from Eric's. He's not there when I arrive, and I only take what I can fit in my duffel, which is pretty much everything. Jules is still not answering her phone, so I make my way back to the hotel. I called Tristan on the way and told him I'm taking a regular room for a while and to take it out of my paycheck. He refused to, but I'll pay him back... eventually.

Just when I didn't think today could get any worse, a familiar car pulls up next to me.

"Jake," my father's voice carries out the window as the car pulls to a stop.

"Hey," I reply with a fake smile. I do not need this right now.

"I've been looking everywhere for you," he says as he exits the car.

Great. I'm not in the mood to talk to him right now. I have a heavy-ass duffle bag on my shoulder, and I've been walking for miles. Eric just kicked me out of his place, and I still can't reach Jules. I just want to throw all this in the hotel room and head to her place to make sure she's okay.

"Can we talk?" he asks, as if I have a choice.

I shrug my shoulders and lead him to a bench close by. Laying the duffle on the ground, I sigh in relief from the weight lifted. At least that's one thing I can fix right now.

"What is it?" I ask, this time not even pretending I'm happy.

He frowns. "Where have you been?"

I shake my head. "Does it matter? You cut me off and told me to leave, so I did."

Seems like nobody really wants me in their life. Funny how easy it is for everyone to just kick me to the curb.

"I told you to come back when you got your life together, not disappear," he says seriously.

I laugh. "Well, that's why I haven't come back. As you can see, my life isn't together."

He looks at the duffle and back at me. "Well, what have you been doing?"

What am I supposed to say? That I've been breaking my back as a housekeeping manager just to survive? He'd only see that as another failure. So instead, I'll give him the answer he expects, because at least that one doesn't cut as deep. Better he looks down on me for something untrue than for the truth that already keeps me up at night.

I roll my eyes, knowing the option I'm always going to choose. "What do you think I've been doing? I've been having a great time. Partying, screwing, and spending time with my buddies."

My father stands up, angry. "When will you learn, Jake? Your mother and brother have been worried about you. Everyone keeps telling me to give you back your job, which I was willing to do, thinking you've learned your lesson."

"What lesson is that, Dad?" I ask, angrily standing up with him.

"That you have to work for what you want and work even harder to keep it. That life isn't about partying and screwing random girls every night. I wanted you to grow up, Jake, and come back ready to run the business and stop being…"

He pauses for too long, so I finish for him. "What dad? Stop being what? Me? I'm sorry that I've always been such a fuck-up to you and everyone else."

I don't need to hear anymore, so I grab my duffle and walk away when his cold voice says, "If you walk away again, Jake, that's it. I'll find someone else to run the company when I'm gone."

I don't even look back as I say, "They can have it."

Rounding the corner of the building, it slams into me… the weight I can't outrun, the darkness I can't fight. Something inside me snaps, and suddenly I'm drowning in it, choking on air that won't fill my lungs. I don't know how much longer I can hold it back. I've been pushing it down for so long, pretending I'm stronger than I am. But the truth is, I'm crumbling.

I thought my life was fucked up before, but now… now it feels completely wrecked. Like I've taken the broken pieces and shattered them even further. What have I done?

My heavy steps finally carry me back to the hotel room, and I toss my duffle onto the bed without care. I make my way to the bar downstairs and down the first whiskey faster than I should have. The burn hits my chest, but it's nothing compared to the knot in my gut. I order a second and nurse it slowly, letting the liquid blur my thoughts as I try to figure out my next steps.

I have a job here that makes decent money. I could work for Tristan higher up for more money, but what's the point? I've lost everything. Right now I don't even care that I lost the company and the ability to go back to my father. All I ever wanted from him was to look at me like he does Bash. I made him so much money and expanded our hotel chain across the country. I did all the hard work, and for what? For some reason, all he sees is a fuck-up when I know I'm not. Yeah, I've made some mistakes, but who hasn't? Nothing that couldn't be fixed.

At least, until today. Did I make a mistake walking away from my father? That can't be fixed. That chapter of my life is gone. And Eric? There's no way he's going to forgive me for screwing his sister behind his back. I betrayed him. I don't deserve his forgiveness. Then there's Jules... I don't even know what's going on there. Is she mad at me? Why isn't she answering my calls or texts? I have a feeling I know the answer. Everyone else leaves me, so why wouldn't she?

I finish off my whiskey and let out a bitter laugh, shaking my head as I head back up to my room. Man, I've fucked up my life. What the hell is wrong with me?

I dig through my duffle, searching for a change of clothes, hoping a hot shower will wash this fucked-up day off me. My hand scrapes against something familiar... a bottle that rattles ominously as I lift it out.

My heart races, betraying me as if it already knows what I'm thinking. I just need to numb everything for a little while... just long enough to wake up and try to piece my life back together. Pulling the bottle out, I open it to find eight pills left. Four pills. That's what I took last time. I woke up fine from a deep sleep. Tonight, with whiskey burning in my veins, four feels safe enough. Or maybe dangerous enough. I'm not sure which I want more.

I should call Rowen. I promised I would if I ever got like this again, but I can't bring myself to do it. He'll talk me down and make me face things I'm not ready to deal with. Right now, I just need everything to stop for a little while. I need a break from the chaos and the darkness in my head. Thinking clearly isn't possible when I'm like this, but maybe in the morning it will be easier.

One thing I do know is that I can't drag Jules down with me any more than I already have. I grab my phone, hesitating only a second before hitting her contact. The dial tone hums in my ear like a countdown. Of course she doesn't answer, so I leave a voicemail.

With my voice barely steady, I say, "Hey Jules... I... I love you. I'm sorry. I won't bother you anymore. Please... just... be happy."

I hang up, my heart pounding and my throat tight. The silence that follows is worse than her answering. It's probably better she didn't, though. I know she's trying to work through things right now too, and I can't help her. I can't help myself right now. It's best that I let her go.

Without a second thought, I swallow the four pills, telling myself it's just enough to take the edge off. I relax on the bed, still fully clothed. I debated taking a shower, but this is better. The whiskey is already helping, and this will allow me to get some decent sleep and hopefully be in a better mindset in the morning.

The room tilts a little. My eyelids are heavy, and my thoughts are sluggish. I laugh softly at myself. I'm supposed to be in control, aren't I? My limbs soften into the bed like it's swallowing me whole. Nodding off mid-thought, I jerk awake, heart pounding. My breathing... shallow. Too shallow. Damn it, it's not supposed to feel like this.

I try to sit up, but I can't. With the floor leaning sideways, everything tilts. My phone screen glows, but the screen is a blur. My name echoes somewhere far away, I think. I'm slipping, and for the first time tonight, fear scratches at my chest.

Chapter Twenty-Six

JULES

After listening to Jake's voicemail, I knew something was wrong. I've been ignoring his calls, but only because I just needed some time to think. I've screwed up everything with my brother and Jake. It's my fault that Eric now hates Jake... and me.

Since Eric kicked him out, I figured he would be at the hotel, but I called Tristan to be sure. He confirmed and gave me his room number. I tried really hard to pretend like nothing was wrong. Was that the right move? I don't know. I feel like something is really wrong.

Jake and I have become well acquainted with each other's bodies, and there's something about his that I haven't had the courage to bring up. Scars mark his wrist that look like cuts. I know he struggles with depression, but I can't stop wondering how deep that struggle goes. How far he would go.

I'm halfway to the hotel when I decide to call Hank. I wasn't going to, but my gut is telling me I should.

"Jules?" he answers on the first ring.

"Hank, hey. I... I think there's something wrong with Jake," I say, not really sure how to explain it.

"What happened?" he asks.

I tell him the situation with my brother, me, and the voice-mail he left.

"Hold on," he says, and the phone goes silent for a moment.

I'm jogging as fast as I can to get to the hotel when Hank comes back to say, "Fuck. He's not answering. How far are you?"

"Like ten minutes," I say, thinking it's too far.

"I'm not in town. I'm sending you his brother's number. Call him and tell him where Jake is," he says.

"What if it's nothing? I could be overreacting," I say.

"No, you're not," he says with a certainty that makes me swallow hard.

"Hank..."

"Jules, I need you to stay calm and just get to him as fast as you can, okay?"

"Okay," I respond, taking a deep breath and begin running.

I want to call hotel security to check on him, but what if I'm wrong? I think Hank is thinking the same thing. I just need to get there and make sure he's okay. He was probably just drunk, and he's hurting. I'm sure he's fine.

I call Bash immediately after hanging up with Hank, explaining who I am and the situation. He says he's on the way, but he's sure Jake's fine. I told him that I'd call him when I got there to let him know. He sounded so sure Jake was just getting drunk and would be okay, while Hank was fearful otherwise. Who should I believe?

Sprinting through the hotel, I snatch the housekeeper room key and race to the room Tristan said he was in, every second dragging, not knowing what I'm about to walk into. I throw the door open.

He's on the bed, his face pale and eyes barely open. My stomach drops. Pills litter the nightstand, and I pick up an empty bottle. I freeze. "Oh God... no..."

Grabbing my phone with trembling fingers, I call his brother back. "He's here... on the bed. Pills... I don't know how many he took... there's only four left from the bottle." My voice cracks.

"Stay calm. I'm almost there," Bash says. I hear the urgency in his tone. Relief flickers but is drowned out immediately by fear.

"Should I call an ambulance?" I ask, ready to hang up and call.

"No, we'll be there faster," he responds, hanging up the phone.

Sinking on the bed beside him, my heart hammers so loud it might as well be a warning siren. He's lying there, pale, half-slumped against the pillows, breathing shallow, eyes fluttering closed. I reach out and brush a lock of hair from his forehead.

"Hey... Jake... wake up," I whisper with a shaky voice. "I'm here. I'm not leaving, okay? You're not alone."

Jake groans, trying to lift his head, but it slumps back. My hand curls over his, holding it tight. Why did he do this? Was it a mistake? Is he trying to kill himself? How could I have been so stupid? Why did I leave him after everything today? I was so selfish. I'm so stupid.

Sobbing, I choke out, "I love you, Jake. I love you. Please don't leave me like this. Hang on."

Tears stream down my cheeks as I sob harder. I need to keep talking to him. I can't let him slip under completely.

"I'm not mad, Jake. You're hurting, and I see it. I love you, all of you, even when it's hard. Even when it's too much. I'm not going anywhere. I'll never go anywhere. Please... just stay with me."

I don't let go of his hand, even when it twitches slightly in response. It's enough for me to know he's still holding on. Every second stretches painfully, and I count them like lifelines until I hear the footsteps running in the hallway. I open the door before they even knock. Bash is finally here.

His brother and another guy move fast, like professionals. Bash kneels beside him, assessing, while the other pulls something from his pocket. Narcan. I hover back, heart in my throat, trying to stay calm.

The first spray hits his nostril. I can only watch as his body jerks, a sharp gasp escaping him. His eyes flutter open, confused and wild. I grab his hand, gripping it like a lifeline.

"I'm here," I whisper, tears continuing to spill. "You're not alone."

He coughs, groans, and swallows hard, still shaky and pale. But alive. I feel this trembling mixture of terror and relief wash over me. He looks confused, and doesn't speak, but I don't care. He's alive.

"Fucking hell, Jake." Bash grabs Jake's head and places his forehead to his.

I back up a little to give him some room, but I keep my hand on Jake's leg. I have to touch him. I need to know that he's okay, and I want him to know I'm here.

"What..." Jake slurs out, still confused.

"Just relax, Jake. Give it a minute," his brother says reassuringly.

Bash looks exactly like his brother, just a little bulkier with shorter hair. He's so calm too. How has he stayed so calm? I'm a mess.

I move to the other side of Jake, so we both can reassure him that we're here and he's not alone, allowing him to come out of his confusion.

After about fifteen minutes, he seems to be coming around, but still weak. He looks... guilty.

"Ah, sorry guys. I fucked up," he mumbles.

Now that Jake seems okay, Bash looks angry. So angry. "What the fuck, Jake? Were you trying to kill yourself?"

Jake shakes his head and only glances at me for a second before looking away. "I didn't mean to... I didn't think..."

Bash interrupts. "Yeah, you didn't think. Fuck. What would've happened if you died, Jake? How..."

The other guy with Bash interrupts, pulling on him. "How about you two step outside for a minute while I take a look and make sure he's okay."

Bash's face relaxes, and I agree. We both step into the hall and let him have a moment with Jake. Whoever he is.

Bash runs his hand through his hair. As if he heard my thoughts, he says, "That's my security guy, Wells."

I nod, but what? Is he super rich and needs security?

"I'm glad that he was here and had Narcan," I reply sincerely.

Bash looks away for a moment, taking a deep breath, rubbing his hand over his face. "Me too. I insisted my security team carry it after... a friend committed suicide the same way. I hate to say it, but if she hadn't... then my brother may not be here today."

I nod, understanding what he's saying. It's shitty that his friend committed suicide, but had she not, then would Bash have insisted his security team carry Narcan? If not, then would Jake be alive? I would have called an ambulance, but would it have been too late?

"What now?" I ask.

Bash leans against the wall, thinking for a moment. "I'm going to take him back to my place and keep an eye on him. Make sure he doesn't relapse. You can come too, if you want."

"Okay. Yeah, I'll see what Jake wants. He might not want me to..." I say, trying to hold back my tears again.

"He loves you, Jules. I've never seen my brother in love before. It's obvious," he reassures me.

"Yeah, but… it's not enough. I… I couldn't help him. He's been in the darkness for so long, I don't know if I'm the one who can pull him out. I have my own demons to fight, and I think they're dragging him down more…" I reply guiltily.

Bash looks at me, confused. "How bad? How bad has he been?"

I shake my head. "He won't show it to anyone, but I see it. I feel it. It's bad. Clearly, it's worse than I thought."

Bash slides down the wall, dropping to the floor with his face in his hands. The strong, composed brother is breaking. He's breaking for Jake. I hate seeing him like this. He looks just like Jake in this moment.

I sit down next to him and wrap him in a hug. I know what he's thinking and feeling because I am too. It sucks.

"It's not your fault, Bash. Jake needs help, and it's more than either of us can give him. It's no one's fault."

Even though I know the words I say are true, they don't reach me. It feels like it's my fault. I pushed him over the edge today. He wouldn't be where he is right now if it weren't for me. We're both drowning in darkness. I hate to say it, but I don't know if we can survive it together.

CHAPTER TWENTY-SEVEN
• • • • • • • • •

JAKE

I feel like shit. Not only from my near miss with death, but for what I just did. Why the fuck did I do that? I don't want to see my brother, and I definitely don't want to see Jules. Wells sent them out of the room to give me space, and I could kiss the guy for it.

He stands against the wall with his arms crossed, watching me as tears stream down my face. Come on. I'm a pussy.

"It's a normal reaction," he says calmly.

I laugh. "Yeah, sure."

He shakes his head and pushes off the wall to sit on the edge of the bed in front of me. "Your body is fighting for its life right now. Just like the shaking, nothing you can do about the crying."

He's probably right. I let the tears go even if he's wrong. I fucked up again. I know I did. That's all I seem to be doing lately. I close my eyes and take a deep breath. What if I had died? Was that my intention? No, I don't think so. I just needed some peace for once. Did I know that was a risk? Of course. And I did it anyway. Fucking stupid.

It would have destroyed Jules. Not just her, but Everly, my brother... Rowen, Ben, James, and everyone else. How could I have been so blind? Why didn't I think about them before taking the pills? That was so selfish. I knew what two glasses of whiskey could do, and still I ignored the consequences. I should have thought. I should have stopped.

"Your brother is going to insist you come back with us to be monitored," he states.

"And probably forever..." I mumble.

Wells smirks at that. "Probably."

I sigh. "He's not going to send me to some rehab facility, is he?"

Wells furrows his brows. "He probably should, but you know he won't if you ask him not to."

Relief spreads through me. Everly confided in me about how her time there went, and it doesn't seem like a good time. Besides, I didn't really try to kill myself. I don't have a death wish. I just want the pain to stop. Either way, I do know I need help. I can't continue like this.

"Are you ready?" he asks, standing up.

I take a deep breath before saying, "Yeah."

Lying on the couch with Bash in the chair beside me, staring at me, makes my skin crawl. Like Wells said, he insisted I come back to his place to be monitored. I didn't put up a fight. Jules offered to come with me, but I didn't want her to have to sit here too. I've caused enough issues in her life, and I'm not going to create more.

"You really don't have to stare at me the entire night," I say joking.

Bash doesn't look impressed. "You tried to kill yourself. I'm not taking my eyes off you."

I cringe at his words. Yeah, it definitely looks like that. "I didn't try to kill myself. It was a mistake."

"A mistake that almost cost you your life," he spits.

He has every right to be angry with me. I almost died. If Jules hadn't heard my voicemail when she did and come to check on me, I'd probably be dead. I could feel it too. My heart rate slowed, and the fear as I was drifting. There was nothing I could do to stop it.

I sit up and stare back at him. "I'm sorry. I know I fucked up again, okay? What do you want from me?"

Bash's face falls. "I just want my brother back."

"What if he doesn't want to come back?" I ask seriously.

"Why? Is life with us so miserable?" he asks, hurt.

I shake my head. "That's not... that's not what I mean."

"Then tell me what you mean," he demands.

At this point, would it hurt? He just found me overdosed on pills and alcohol. Nothing is worse than that.

"Alright, then, the truth. I'm fucking depressed, and I have been my entire life. I've been pretending to be okay, to be happy, to be the Jake you've known. I'm not him, though. Fuck, I don't even know who I am. At least, until I met Jules. I could be myself. I don't have to pretend with her, and I genuinely, for once in my life, felt happy. I don't want to go back to the person I was before. He never truly existed," I say, looking away from him.

We're both silent for a few minutes until he breaks it. "I... I didn't know Jake. I did, but I didn't. Why didn't you tell me before? Suffering from depression isn't a crime. You're not weak because of it. We could've gotten you help sooner."

I laugh. "Really? Dad made his stance on mental health issues clear."

Bash shakes his head. "Dad's an idiot. Screw him."

I take a moment to think before speaking. I'm not sure if I should be completely open or not with him. Will he look at me differently if I am?

"I'm not who everyone thinks I am, and I hate it. I'm not some frat party boy who hooks up with random girls all the time. I hate that image. Yeah, I've partied, but only to drown out the depressing thoughts in my head. And girls? I can count on both hands how many I've been with. Hell, I wasn't with anyone after Everly and I ended our friends-with-benefits arrangement in Georgia."

Bash looks surprised. "Seriously? Not a single girl since then? That's like over four years ago."

I shrug my shoulders. "Well, obviously, Jules, but that's it. I worked my butt off for Dad too, but he could never see me for anything other than the image he had in his head."

"Why did you let us think those things then, Jake?" he asks seriously.

"It was easier. I would rather be known for that than the spoiled rich kid who claims to be depressed."

"Depression doesn't discriminate. It doesn't matter if you have five dollars or five billion. No friends or an army of friends. Abusive parents or loving ones. When the darkness finds you, it will chase you, no matter who you are or what your circumstances are. I can't claim to know exactly how it feels, but I do know this... there's no way to fight it alone... you'll never win. And brother, you're not alone. You have an army at your back to help you face your demons. We'll never let you battle this alone again," he says sincerely.

I don't respond. Not that I don't want to, but I can't. Tears stream down my face, and I don't care this time. My brother knew exactly what to say to me. He does know me. I always feel so guilty whenever the depression takes hold because I don't deserve to be depressed. My life is amazing compared to the majority of people in this world.

I always question why I'm depressed when I have so much going for me, but he's right. It doesn't matter how much I have. It's going to find me. So, here's where I have to make a choice. I can either let it keep finding me and battle it alone, or I can fight it with the help of my friends and family.

CHAPTER TWENTY-EIGHT

JULES

I find myself standing outside my brother's apartment door, trying to gather the courage to knock. After Jake told me he didn't want me to go back with him and his brother, I wandered the streets aimlessly, unsure where to go. The thought of returning to my place, to that empty silence, felt unbearable.

Once the rain began to pour, I found myself walking toward Eric's place. He might turn me away, but right now, I need him. I'm still sobbing and drenched as I finally find the courage to knock on his door.

It only takes a few seconds for him to open the door and process the state I'm in.

"Jules?" he asks, concerned.

I sob even harder, throwing myself at him, as he wraps me in his arms.

"Hey, it's okay. Come in and tell me what's going on," he says soothingly, which makes me sob even harder.

He guides me toward the couch before disappearing into his bedroom. I sink down, hating myself for showing up here. I don't deserve his kindness, not after the months I've spent pushing him away, lying to his face. But the truth is, I have nowhere else to go. No one else to turn to.

He comes back into the room with a towel, T-shirt and shorts for me to change into. I stop crying long enough to take them from him. I'm so drained, I don't even care about changing in front of him versus going to the bathroom. Giving me privacy, he grabs me some water, and once I'm done changing, he pulls me to his side where I start crying again.

"Jules... talk to me," he pleads.

I cry out, "Jake almost died, and it's my fault."

"What?!" he asks, shocked.

I cry even harder in his chest as he asks, "What happened? Where is he?"

I take a deep breath and try to hold back my tears as I sit straight. "I left after you did and ignored his calls. He needed me, and I just left him. He... He took too many pills..."

It's so hard to continue, but I push through. "I found him in the hotel... I almost lost him, Eric. He almost died. If I hadn't found him in time..."

"But you did, right? You found him in time?" he asks, concerned for Jake.

I nod. "His brother came, and they had Narcan. He's at his house now. He didn't want me to go with them. I don't blame him. He doesn't want me anymore."

Eric pulls me in for another hug. "Jesus Jules. I'm sorry."

He pauses another moment before continuing. "I don't think it's that he doesn't want you. He probably feels guilty and embarrassed. He didn't want you to see him that way. He loves you, Jules. Fuck, I didn't even know who he was seeing, but I could tell how much he loved her."

I cringe at his words. "I'm sorry I didn't tell you. I didn't want you to be mad at me. I've screwed up so much, I didn't want to do it again."

"You didn't screw anything up, Jules. The accident wasn't your fault, and I'm not mad at you for that. I was angry that you didn't tell me. Then you kept dating Jake a secret..."

"I know," I interrupt.

He shakes his head. "No, let me continue. I'm always here for you. You're my sister, and I hate that you felt you needed to keep all that from me. I just want you to be happy, and I want to be there for you when life throws you curveballs. I can't be though if you're keeping secrets from me."

"I didn't want to disappoint you," I whisper.

"You'll never disappoint me. I love you, Jules," he replies, pulling me into another hug.

"I love you too," I say back.

Eric spends the next hour calming me and reassuring me that Jake is going to be okay with his brother and that he will still want me. Then we spend time catching up on everything we've missed in each other's lives, and he assures me he's not upset with me anymore. I'm thankful he's so forgiving because I don't know what I'd do without him.

I wanted to call Jake to make sure that he's doing okay, but I know Eric's right that his brother is taking care of him. If he needs some time to figure things out, then I'll have to give it to him. I just want to be with him, but I know that's not the best thing for him right now. Being with family is.

Jake and I both have our own demons, and when we're together, it feels like we can push them aside. We comfort each other, yes, but neither of us wants to face what's inside. We have to confront our darkness apart, or we'll drown together in it. And that scares me. What happens when we've worked on ourselves, when we're in a better place? Will we still want each other then? Or will he look at me and realize he doesn't need me anymore?

It's been a week since that horrible night with Jake. A week since I've talked to him. A week since I've seen him. A week since I've felt even remotely whole. A week can be so damn long.

Eric and I worked out our differences, and now we talk on the phone every day. When he said he would have been happy for Jake and me to be together, I could tell he truly meant it. He clearly cares for Jake, and the friendship they've formed took him by surprise. Living with Jake for a while has shown him that Jake is a good guy, and he trusts that I'm safe with him.

Jake hasn't shown up at work. In fact, he quit. Tristan called me into his office to talk to me about it and wanted to assure me I still have a job there for as long as I want. Of course I thanked him, and I plan to stay here for a little while longer, but not forever.

During one of my many conversations with Eric, I told him about my dream of opening an affordable dance studio for children. He loves the idea and wants to support me. Apparently, his ex, Everly, gave him a substantial amount of money when she left, but he never touched it. She gave it to him because she genuinely cared about him and wanted him to succeed in life. Honestly, it sounds like pity money to me. I understand why he said he didn't want it, but he kept it just in case of an emergency with me or our parents. Now he wants to use some of it to help me get started. I haven't accepted yet, but I'm leaning toward it.

So, this week has been about getting my life in order and making plans for the future. I actually feel good about everything, and things are looking up. I finally told my parents about my accident, and they were also really upset that I kept it from them but not mad about it happening. They just want to be there for me, like Eric. They plan to visit again soon, and this time I'm looking forward to it.

Now, the one thing still bringing me down... Jake. I don't know where we stand. He hasn't texted or called once. I haven't either. His brother has texted me daily with updates that he's fine, but that's about all I get. Bash also told me that he took Jake's phone, which makes me feel a little better. I'm trying not to be selfish, but it hurts a little that Jake hasn't wanted to talk to me at all. I found him almost dead, and that's after my brother told me to have a good life. I would've thought he'd want to make sure I'm okay.

I shake those thoughts away as I walk out of the hotel after my shift. As I'm walking home, a familiar figure steps beside me.

"Hey Jules," he says quietly.

I smile at him. "Hey Hank. What are you doing here?"

"Let's go to dinner," he states versus asking.

Well, that's random. I think about it for a moment, but at the mention of dinner, my stomach decides to let out a loud growl. I laugh because I know he heard it.

"Sure."

We pop into a restaurant close by and sit at a booth in the back corner where no one can see us. Weird. I noticed he's also wearing a hat and sunglasses, like he doesn't want anyone to know that he's here.

"How are you doing?" he asks.

I give him a reassuring smile. "I'm doing good. Finally figuring my life out."

He studies me for a moment before saying, "Good. You look good."

"What about you? How are you?" I ask.

He looks at me like that's the strangest question he's ever heard. "Good."

Okay... Does no one ever ask him how he's doing? My heart sinks. I hope that's not the case. That would be such a lonely life to think no one cares enough about you to ask you a simple question like that.

He breaks me out of my thoughts and says, "Jake's doing good. He wanted me to check on you myself. Your brother has kept him updated that you're good, but he knew that I would tell him the truth."

Wait, my brother has been talking to him?

As if Hank knows what I'm thinking, he says, "Eric texts Bash. Bash is keeping Jake on a tight leash right now."

"But he also talked to you..." I say, still feeling hurt.

"Nah. Bash was on the phone with me, and he stole it to tell me to check on you."

I laugh at the image of him doing that. "So are they keeping him prisoner or something? I don't feel like that's going to help him..."

Hank shakes his head. "No. Jake insisted, actually. He wants to figure things out, and get better before he comes back to you."

My breath hitches. He comes back to me. So he still wants me. That thought is enough to give me hope, to make my chest feel lighter. I'm so glad Hank showed up and insisted we get dinner. I'm glad Jake still cares enough to send him to check on me.

Dinner goes by quickly as we talk about random things, and I even got Hank to laugh a few times. I like him and can see why Jake is friends with him. I also talked to him about my ideas for the dance studio. He was excited to hear about it and said he'd love to make donations to it once it's up and running. I'm thankful because that's going to be a crucial part of keeping it open and providing affordable or free classes for those who can't afford it.

Hank walked me back to my place to ensure I got home safely. As I head into my apartment, I still miss Jake like crazy, but I'm feeling hopeful. I'm hopeful that Jake is getting the help he needs, and that I'm getting my life in order, so that when we next see each other, we can officially be a couple and move on together.

CHAPTER TWENTY-NINE

JAKE

A whole month has dragged by since I last saw Jules. Every day has been torturous, each hour stretching longer than the one before, but it was necessary. I had to get my life together before I could face her again. She's the last one on my list, only because I can't risk screwing this up with her. I love her. I need her.

I've spent all month figuring out my next steps and talking to everyone in my life. I made Bash take my phone away and basically keep me prisoner, monitoring who comes and goes. I needed to ensure that I only talked to one person at a time rather than overwhelming myself with everyone I needed to talk to and everything I needed to do.

In the first week, I finally found help. Bash had a therapist come in every day to talk to me, and I was also prescribed depression medication. At first, I didn't feel like it helped, but after a few weeks, I'm noticing a huge difference. I feel alive. I genuinely feel happy without pretending or forcing myself to.

It's been damn hard keeping my distance from Jules, but I just hope she understands. One day that first week, I was going crazy thinking about her. I know Bash updated her about me and Eric told Bash she was doing well, but I still worried. When I overheard Bash on the phone with Rowen, or as he knows him, Hank, I stole the phone right out of his hand. I only had a few seconds to get the words out, but he understood the assignment. Bash told me Hank went to dinner with her, and she's doing really well. I'm glad, but I hope that she hasn't forgotten about me.

Everly was the first person I saw, and it was hard. I decided it was best to be open with everyone in my life, just like I was with Bash. I told her everything. She cried so hard, and so did I. I feel awful that I almost left her like that, but I'm grateful I'm here. I thought she would be a little bit pissed at me, but she wasn't at all. Just concerned. Out of everyone, I knew she'd be the most understanding.

James was next, but I wasn't as open with him as I was with Everly and Bash. I figured she would tell him the details. James was a little mad that I've been keeping everything to myself, but ultimately, he was just happy I'm still here. It ended with a hug and a promise that I'd come to him for anything in the future. He'd keep whatever it is between us if needed, even from Everly. That made me want to cry because even with our differences in the past, he still cares about me.

Ben was a mess, and I wanted to push him right back out the door to make him stop. Before leaving my life behind, Ben was the one I spent most of my time with. He's been my best friend since we were kids. We were meeting at a bar or hanging out at one of our places weekly. He felt awful that he hadn't realized how bad my depression was, but how could he have? I had years of experience pretending. Of everyone, I think he's taking this the hardest.

I wasn't looking forward to talking with Rowen, so I was going to avoid him as much as possible. Of course, the first time I stepped outside, he happened to be there. I'm surprised that he risked being seen, especially with security on me. He didn't stay long as he just wanted to see that I was alright and let me know he wasn't mad at me. That he was here for me, as always.

I've been feeling so alone most of my life, and I don't even know why. After talking to everyone and seeing how much they actually care about me, I feel stupid. I think I was just brought up feeling like no one cared because of the way my parents were. My dad has always made comments about how stupid this mental health crap is, whatever that means. We never really talked about our feelings with each other. I just assumed no one would care, but I was wrong. The important people in my life care. That's all I need.

I take a deep breath as I'm about to walk into my childhood home. The last visit before I see Jules is with my parents. I don't expect much to come of this, but I need closure. Be it that my father still hates me and kicks me out of his life for good along with his company or not. Either way, it needs to be done so I can finally move on and see Jules again.

One of the housekeepers lets me into the house, and I find my mother waiting just inside the door. The moment she sees me, she rushes forward, tears glistening in her eyes, and pulls me into a hug. I hug her back and let myself melt into her warmth. She's never been much of a hugger, so this sudden closeness catches me off guard.

She pulls away and cups my face as she says, "Come now. I have your favorite cookies, and your father is waiting in the living room."

I swallow hard and walk with her to the living room, finding my father typing on his laptop. The moment he sees me, he places it down, clears his throat, and walks over to... hug me? Yeah, he's hugging me.

"I'm sorry, son," he says.

I'm choked up, so I don't respond. Did my father really just hug me and apologize?

We all sit, my mother beside me and my father across from me. No one's saying anything, and I don't know what to say. Everything I had planned in my head was going to be in response to anger, frustration, and them not understanding or caring. I never considered I'd get hugs and an apology from my father.

My mother grabs my hand and looks at me with sadness in her eyes. "Jake... I'm so sorry I never noticed. I feel like such a terrible mother for not knowing."

I shake my head. "No, Mom. You couldn't have noticed. It's not your fault."

She sighs. "I should have noticed, and I should've been honest with you."

Honest with me? About what?

She continues. "I suffer from depression too. I've been on medication for almost a year now, and it has helped greatly. Depression can run in families, and I should've seen it sooner. You had all the signs. You were just like me, but you hid it so much better."

I'm shocked. "What? I never knew you had depression..."

She laughs. "Why do you think I was such a terrible mother to you both?"

"You weren't..." I start, but she interrupts.

"Yes, I was. I didn't know it back then, but I had horrible postpartum depression with both of you boys, and it continued to get worse through the years. Whenever I was depressed, I would get more down because I knew I wasn't the mother you needed. I thought distancing myself from my family and friends would help, but it made it worse. I just... I didn't know how to handle it and before I knew it, you boys were grown up and out of the house... I'm sorry I was never the mother you needed me to be," she says with tears in her eyes.

Wow. Wow... I never knew. She was distant and never super affectionate, but I just thought that was her. I didn't love her any less. I can't believe I didn't notice.

"That's not true, and I'm sorry I didn't know. I wish I had known," I trail off.

"Me too," she says with a sad smile.

My father clears his throat, looking at my mom. She nods before he says, "I take responsibility too. I know I've been vocal about mental health disorders, but I didn't know… I never experienced it, and that doesn't make it okay…"

My father pauses, but I can tell he has more to say. Whatever it is, it's going to be hard to hear.

He continues. "Last summer was an eye-opener for me. Your mother got bad, about to the point you were last month. It put things into perspective for me. We got her the help she needed, and I wanted to be more present in her life. I've been planning to retire sooner to spend more time with her, you boys, and hopefully my future grandchildren."

I look at my mom and close my eyes to process. Shit. How had I not noticed at all? I was so consumed in my own darkness I didn't see hers. How did I not? I see it in everyone, but I guess she's just always had it that I couldn't see the difference. This is why my dad has been on my case more? He just wanted to ensure that I was ready to take over the business so he could retire sooner. I feel like a jerk.

My father continues, breaking the silence. "Jake… had I known you were suffering too… I wouldn't have been so hard on you. I just thought…"

He trails off, so I finish for him. "You thought I was a spoiled rich kid taking daddy's money and having fun? Yeah, I know. That's the image I preferred you to see. Versus the spoiled rich kid who was depressed for no reason."

My mom shakes her head. "No Jake. You can't look at it like that. There doesn't have to be a reason."

"I know. I know that now. I just didn't want to burden anyone," I say truthfully.

"You'll never be a burden, son. I hope that you're getting the help you need and know that we're here for you too. The company is yours when you're ready to return," my father says sincerely.

Out of all the outcomes I prepared for before coming over here, I never expected this. It's the best possible one.

"So... we hear there's a girl. Tell us about her," my mom changes the topic.

I smile and talk about Jules for the rest of my visit. It's hard not to talk about her. I miss her so damn much. I just hope I didn't fuck it up with her because I don't know how I'm going to live without her. I know it'll be an adjustment going back to my old life and incorporating her into it, but it'll be worth it. I know she's it for me. I just hope I'm the only one for her.

Chapter Thirty

JULES

Ugh, today was a hard day at work. I'm ready to get out of here and start my dance studio. Spaces have been on my radar, but nothing feels quite right yet. Maybe nothing ever will. I think I've been holding off until things are figured out with Jake. I miss him so much, but I know he needs this time for himself. I needed the time too.

I pull the hood of my raincoat up as I step out of the hotel doors. Just as it settles over my head, I catch sight of him, Jake, leaning against the wall. My heart stops. I blink, do a double take, but he's still there.

I move toward him slowly, even though every part of me wants to run, to throw myself into his arms and never let go. But I don't know if he wants that. So I hold myself back, trying to play it cool while my pulse hammers in my chest. Every step feels like torture. He's only a few feet away, yet it feels like an eternity to close the distance.

"Hey," I say, forcing a smile as I finally reach him.

He smiles back softly. "Hey."

"Hi." The word slips out before I can stop it, and I immediately groan inside at how ridiculous I sound.

He chuckles. "Want to grab some dinner?"

"Yes!" I say a little too excitedly.

Damn it, I want to hug him so badly. To kiss him. To do something! But I don't know why he's here. Is he here to officially break up with me? Is he here to tell me he needs more time? Is he here because he missed me as much as I missed him?

"I missed you, Jules," he says, tentatively reaching for my hand.

I let out the breath I was holding and grab his hand, squeezing it tight. "I missed you too."

We walk silently, hand in hand, to our favorite go-to restaurant. I miss this. I miss being near him. I miss everything about him.

When we make it inside, our usual server takes our orders and is excited to see us after all the time that has passed. I have to say I'm happy to see her too.

"How are you?" Jake asks me after she leaves.

"I'm doing good, actually. What about you?" I ask, hoping he really is doing as well as he looks.

"I'm doing great. I got the support I needed, and started some medication, which has really made a difference. I feel like I have almost everything in my life figured out," he says.

"That's great, Jake. What haven't you figured out?" I ask, but my heart races for his response.

"You."

"What about me?" I ask hopefully.

"You're the only person I've been thinking about day and night this past month. I wanted to see you so badly, but I knew I couldn't. I needed to get my life in order because I want you to be part of it. I can't see a future without you, Jules, and I hope you'll forgive me for everything. I'm sorry I wasn't able to be there for you when you needed it most, too. I feel awful for that..."

I interrupt him with tears in my eyes. "No, Jake. You don't have to apologize. I'm just so happy you're okay. And... I want that too. I couldn't stop thinking about you either. I want to be in your life too. I want to meet your friends and family. I want to be part of your good and bad days. I want it all with you."

"You mean that?" he asks, looking shocked.

"Yes."

He lets go of my hand, stands up, and pushes me further into the booth so he can sit next to me. He grabs my face and kisses me hard. I sigh with the relief that floods through me as he kisses me. I missed him so much.

He pulls away, laughing. "Sorry, I couldn't wait another second."

I laugh too. "I'm glad you didn't, because I couldn't either."

He kisses me again before heading back to his side of the booth.

"So... I guess this means I need to be honest with you," he says.

I look at him confused. "About what?"

"My life… So, my family is… rich. I'm supposed to be taking over my father's company…" Jake trails off as though it's a bad thing.

"Like, how rich?" I ask, but I have a feeling I know.

After I met Jake's brother and saw he had security with him, I kind of googled him… and obviously that turned up some results about Jake too. I didn't look at much because I didn't want to learn about him from the internet, which I know is false. The moment I saw an article about him going home with a new girl on his arm after every event, I closed it. Not because I was jealous, but I knew it wasn't true.

"Billions?" he asks like he's unsure how I'd react.

"Huh… interesting," I say but don't elaborate.

"What?" he asks.

I shrug my shoulders.

"You have to give me something, Jules."

I laugh. "What do you think I'm going to say to that Jake? Oh my gosh, I can't be with a billionaire? How dare you keep this from me and let us both work gross jobs to make ends meet? Oh yay, can we get married now?" I say all this in a high-pitched, sweet voice.

Jake laughs. "I don't know. I didn't know how you'd take it."

I look at him seriously now. "Jake… I meant what I said. I'd love you even if we were poor and housekeepers for the rest of our lives. Of course, I'm going to love you when you're rich. I would have run away with you and started a whole new life with you. I'll do and have whatever, Jake, as long as you're by my side."

He clears his throat as our food arrives. He's looking at me as if he's never seen me before. As though he can't believe that I'm real.

"Jules?" he asks.

"Yeah?"

"Do you mean all that? Would you want to marry me?" he asks.

I laugh. "Yes Jake. If you asked right now, I'd say yes. But I think first we should probably get to know each other in your world. I'd like to officially meet your brother and all your friends. If you want me to, that is."

He nods. "I want you to. They've been dying to meet you. And just so you know, I will be asking you to marry me, but it's going to be an extravagant proposal. I need some time to come up with something perfect."

I laugh again. "Jake, you know that I'd be happy if you just got down on one knee at this restaurant."

He cringes. "Ew, do you really want me to kneel on this filthy floor?"

We both laugh because he's obviously kidding. Just a few months ago, he was cleaning up vomit and other bodily fluids in hotel rooms with me. It's crazy to think about how much has changed since we met on that first day. We were both so consumed with darkness that we felt hopeless. Now there's so much hope for our future. Our future. Together.

After dinner, Jake insists on driving me back to his place. His place from his old life. He wanted me to see it because he said I'll be living there soon too. I get into the car with his driver, Stan. He seems nice.

"You'd better get used to this," Jake says.

"What?" I ask.

He laughs. "This. You're going to be driven everywhere you go. I'm not letting you walk to work. Which you should probably go ahead and quit. You don't need to work there anymore."

I look at him confused. "What do you mean? I can't just quit my job."

He cocks an eyebrow at me. "You're dating a billionaire."

I shrug. "So? And what if that billionaire decides to kick my ass to the curb?"

Jake laughs this time and leans in close to my ear. "The only thing I'll be doing to your ass is fucking it." He leans back in his seat, grinning at my blushing. "Jules, you're stuck with me now. Now that I've sorted my shit out, I'm going to take care of you. Every need or want you have... it's yours."

"Jake..." I start, but don't get a chance to finish.

"Jules, I'm not taking no for an answer. Unless after seeing my life and the whole me you don't want me anymore, then I'm not letting you go. You're mine."

You're mine. I never thought I'd like hearing those words and being someone's possession, but coming from Jake, I love it. I want to hear it every day. I want to be his, and I want him to be mine. Forever.

Chapter Thirty-One

JAKE

After showing Jules my penthouse apartment, I insisted she stay the night. I wanted to insist she stay forever, but I know I need to give her time to adjust to everything. Plus, she hasn't met my friends yet, which she's about to do soon. All of them. At once. If this doesn't scare her off, then I know she'll stay for good.

Before that, I have one more person I need to see. I said I was saving Jules for last, but technically that's a lie. I needed to see how Jules felt about me after this month before I paid him a visit.

My heart races as I knock on his door. I hear footsteps inside, so I know he's home. The door opens a moment later.

"Hey, Eric... can we talk?" I ask nervously.

Eric nods and holds the door open for me to come in.

My heart's racing, palms sweaty. I feel like I'm about to ask the guy to marry his sister, which I suppose basically I am because that's the endgame. Jules and I will be married one day.

Hopefully sooner rather than later, but I'm not going to push her. As long as she's in my life, I'll be happy.

Eric leads me to the living room, and we both sit down. Okay, this is good. He didn't outright slam the door in my face or punch me.

I clear my throat. "Eric... I'm sorry."

There's a whole list of things I want to say sorry for, but by the look on his face, he understands. Thank God I don't have to go down the entire list because we'd be here forever.

"You're doing alright?" Eric asks.

I'm surprised that's the first thing out of his mouth. "Yeah, I'm great."

He tilts his head while inspecting me. "For real and not pretend?"

I smirk. "For real. I've gotten help, and I'm doing well."

He nods. "I'm glad. You scared me, you know."

"Really?" I ask surprised.

Eric takes his glasses off and rubs his hand over his face before responding. "Yeah, of course. Jake... You've become one of my closest friends. I care about you."

"That means more to me than you know..." I say aloud even though I meant to say it to myself.

Taking a deep breath in, Eric says, "I'm sorry about how I reacted. I was just hurt that I was being lied to by both my friend and sister."

"I didn't want to lie to you," I say sincerely.

He nods. "I know. Jules has made it quite clear that it was her, and you wanted to tell me. You didn't because you were trying to do what she wanted and what was best for her, and I appreciate that more than anything."

"So you're not mad that I'm with her?" I ask skeptically.

Eric laughs. "No, I'm not mad that you're with her. I've had all month to think about it, and Jake, you're exactly who I would want for her. I've seen a different side of you since you moved in here, and I've heard the way you talk about her. The way you love her. Obviously I didn't know it was her, but that's exactly what I've always hoped my sister would find."

I grin and let out a sigh. "Oh good. I'm so glad that you approve because family events would've been awkward."

Eric smiles and shakes his head. "Family events will definitely be entertaining with you around."

"Oh, they will be. You know, I used to be quite the prankster. It's been a while, but I think I still have it in me."

Eric laughs again. "Oh, I remember. Everly shared a lot of stories with me."

I laugh thinking about Everly and my pranks, but then my mind quickly drifts to other places. What if Jules doesn't like who I am in my world? What if Jules decides she can't handle being in my world? What if she hates my friends?

"What's going on in that mind of yours, Jake?" Eric asks.

I wonder for a moment if I should tell him, and decide why not? He is my friend and, hopefully, one day, my brother-in-law. We should be able to be honest with each other and give advice.

"I'm worried Jules might not like the real me, my world, or my friends," I say seriously.

"Yeah, that's not going to happen. Jules is head over heels for you, man."

"How can you be so sure?" I ask.

Eric laughs. "Really? She's my sister, and do you know how often she talked about you this past month? Every. Damn. Day."

I lean back and relax a little. "That makes me feel a little better. I just worry because it's been us against the world, in our own little bubble. Now we're introducing my entire world, and my friends can be... a lot."

Eric shrugs. "She's dealt with crappy people her whole life in the competition world, so I think she can handle your welcoming friends and family.... Though... Everly might be a challenge..."

I cock my eyebrow. "What do you mean?"

Grimacing, he says, "Well... she liked her fine when we were together, but she hated her because of what happened between us..."

Ouch. I didn't even think about that. Shit. Everly is one of my best friends. I can imagine Jules hates her because what happened between her and Eric wasn't pretty. Eric loved Everly with everything he had, and she didn't love him back the same way. From Jules' point of view, it looks like Everly strung him along, dumped him, and then got married to someone else... who she never stopped loving. Ugh.

I groan. "What do I do about that?"

Eric shrugs. "I'd warn her first, but just be patient. Jules can hold grudges, but she loves you and will try for you. Plus, Everly is great, and she'll see that once she gets to know her."

"Yeah, you're right," I say, but now I'm concentrating on something else.

The way he said Everly is great was different from how he normally talks about her. Usually there's longing in his eyes and pain in his words. This time, it was just a compliment about her character.

I lean forward. "So, what's been going on in your life that I've missed? Anyone new?"

Eric looks away and back again with a grin on his face. "Kind of."

"Kind of?" I chuckle.

He shrugs. "I may have been dating someone this past month."

"Where'd you meet?"

"At your brother's event," he replies.

"Oh!! It's Sierra, isn't it?" I ask, remembering him talking to her.

"How'd you know?" He looks surprised.

Laughing, I say, "I saw the way you two were hitting it off. That's why I left you alone."

"Yeah, it's complicated though. She helped me get a job at your brother's company the following week, and she's technically my boss..."

"Huh. Bash didn't mention hiring you," I say.

Eric laughs. "Dude, he had no idea. I ran into him on the elevator one day, and he was shocked to see me and hear about me working there."

I can't help but laugh at that. My brother has so much trust in the people he hires. He doesn't hire anyone he can't trust to do a job without his approval for everything. Unless it's directly under him or someone he's going to be interacting with daily, then he doesn't care who his team chooses to hire.

It does make me curious about what Bash thinks about Eric working there, though. I have a feeling he would have immediately called Everly to make sure she was okay with it. Of course she would be. While she didn't love Eric the way she loves James, she still loved him. She wants what's best for him.

Eric and I finish catching up, and I'm so thankful that I didn't screw our relationship up. I really like him. It's weird to think of how we've gotten to where we are today. We met as he was falling for Everly, and I was trying to get over her. Then he threw me a bone when I had nothing, and soon, he'll be my brother-in-law. Damn, this world is crazy.

As I'm heading out, I say, "Don't renew your lease next month."

"What?" he asks, confused.

Grinning, I pat him on the shoulder as I say, "I owe you for everything you've done for me. There's an apartment in my building for lease, so it's going to be yours."

He shakes his head. "There's no way I can afford that, Jake."

"Seriously, Eric? What part of I owe you don't you understand? Your sister is going to want you close by, and she's going to be living with me soon. I'm paying for the apartment."

"And what if you two break up? Then I'm stuck with something I can't afford."

Shaking my head, I say, "And if we break up, then I'm still paying because you're my friend. You saved my life, Eric, and for that I can never repay you. Just take it for now, save up, and if you want to move out eventually to get a house and start a family, do that. But for now, let me repay you and make my future wife happy in the meantime."

Before Eric can object any more, I walk out the door and close it behind me with a smile on my face. Life is good. Life is so fucking good, and I thank God I didn't fuck it up that night with my stupidity.

CHAPTER THIRTY-TWO

JULES

Jake's life is nothing like I ever imagined. When I first met him months ago, I never would've believed he could command a city the way he does. And yet I know I've only seen the edges of his world, just the surface of everything he carries.

This past week, being back in his life, has been incredible, like a piece of me I didn't even realize was missing finally clicked back into place. It's overwhelming, yes, and I know it'll take time to adjust to all of it. But I'm here. I'm not going anywhere.

I've only stayed one night at his place. Not because I didn't want to, but because I'm just not ready yet. He's been asking me to move in, and while he isn't pushy about it, I know he wants me there. I know one day I will be, but right now, I need to get to know this Jake before I can take a step that big.

The Jake I first met was charming, funny, a little lost, still trying to figure out who he was and where he was going. This new Jake... he's still all of those things, but there's a quiet confidence in him now. He carries himself with the certainty of knowing exactly what he wants, and exactly how to get it. And I won't lie, it's sexy.

"Jules," Jake says from behind me, making me jump.

"Geez Jake. Stop sneaking up on me." I place my hand over my racing heart to calm it.

He laughs. "I texted you, knocked on the door, and made a bunch of noise coming in."

Shaking my head, I respond, "Yeah, well... clearly that wasn't enough."

He walks up behind me and wraps his arms around me, kissing my neck. I moan and melt into his touch. It amazes me how easily this man can make me forget the world exists when he's here.

I turn around and kiss him. "You know... it's been a while since..."

He places his finger over my lips and scrunches his face like he's in pain. "Jules, I want you so badly, but now is not the time."

I laugh. "Are you sure? We can be a little late. It's been a while... I don't think it'll take long..."

He interrupts me by pressing his lips to mine, but it's not a passionate kiss. It's gentle. As quickly as it comes, it's gone.

"No fair..." I say.

Jake laughs. "If after today you still want to, then you're spending the night with me at my place. I'm not having sex with you again until you agree to stay over."

I gasp. "What?! You would withhold sex from me to get what you want?"

Jake looks at me seriously. "That's not... Jules, I fucking love you, and you know where I stand. Now I need to know where you stand after today. If you're all in, knowing my world's a little crazy."

I kiss him again, but don't push for anything more. He's right. I kind of feel bad for making him feel like I'm not completely all in yet. I know I am. I am... but... I don't know what the but is. It's just all so different. It's scary.

"Hey, you don't have to make a decision today, okay? I told you I just want you to get to know my world. We're still just dating, and at any point if this isn't what you want... you're free to leave."

Wow. I don't know why, but those words hurt. Maybe because I know I can't survive anymore without him. I can't imagine leaving. That whole month without him, I was miserable. No matter what, this is going to work between us. I want to tell him that, but I don't.

"Come on, let's go. It's time you met everyone in my life," he says, holding his hand out to me, and I take it.

Oh my God. This isn't anything like I thought it would be, meeting his friends. I don't know what I expected, but... not this. I can see why Jake needed some space from his world and all of them. It has been a lot from the moment I walked in the front door. It's not bad, it's good. It's great. It's amazing. It's just... a lot.

I sneak off to the bathroom to get a breather. We're at his brother's apartment or penthouse, whatever. It's beautiful, and I can't even imagine living in a place like this. Then again, Jake's isn't that far off from this. Jake's is a little less... extravagant, but still ridiculous.

Bash is really nice, and I can tell he cares about his brother just like Eric cares about me. His fiancée is even nicer, Amelia. She's gorgeous, and I'm kind of jealous I don't have red hair like she does. I can tell we're going to be good friends already. She's obviously not from money, just like me.

Jake's friend, Ben, is super sweet as well, and hot. It amazes me how good-looking all his friends are. It's crazy, but no one compares to Jake. I still can't believe how lucky I am to have landed him. Anyway, Ben is kind, and I can tell he's the type of friend that would do anything for you. He's a little awkward though, like the hug he gave me when I came in.

James is also really nice. I think they said he's Ben's brother, but he doesn't look anything like him. I can tell he's the serious and practical friend. Which is funny because he's the complete opposite of Jake. I think that's the one Jake said he had a falling out with for a few years, and my heart squeezes at thinking about why that may be.

Everly... seeing her here was a shock. Jake had wanted to warn me, but I told him not to. I thought I could handle whatever came without preparation. Now I understand the hesitation in his eyes back then, and I wish I'd let him tell me because standing here, I'm a mess of confusion and mixed feelings.

It's clear she cares about Jake, and from the way they move around each other, they're closer than I realized. And that leaves me with too many questions that I'll have to carry until I get the chance to ask him. And then there's the past, the tangled history with her and Eric. I know I'll have to let it go, put it to rest once and for all. Especially since Eric seems happy now with Sierra.

I also met a couple of their security guards. Declan and Ryder belong to James and Everly. I'm not sure who goes with who though. Wells' is Bash's and... I cannot for the life of me remember the name of Amelia's. I'll have to ask her again. Stan brought us here, but he didn't walk us inside like the rest of them did. I wonder why they all seem really crazy about security, but Jake is more relaxed? I didn't see one for Ben either.

I splash water on my face and pat it dry, staring at myself in the mirror. Ugh. Okay. Time to go back out there. I can do this. This is fine. Everyone's been kind. No one's treated me badly. It's just... it's going to take time. I've been on my own for so long that being surrounded by people feels foreign, like I'm wearing skin that doesn't quite fit. But for Jake, I'll push through and try.

The moment I walk out of the bathroom, I'm met with a pregnant stomach and an unsure smile. Everly stands in front of me like she's been waiting for me.

"It's a lot, isn't it?" she asks.

I chuckle. "Yeah, it is."

Her smile fades as she asks, "Can we talk?"

I nod and follow her down the hall to a room that looks like a mix of a library and office. It's cute, and I wonder if this is where Amelia spends a lot of her time.

Everly closes the door behind us and says, "Let's sit for a minute. I just wanted to say a few things."

My heart is racing. Is this the moment she tells me I don't belong in her world? That she and Jake were more than friends, that they were in love? I don't know if I could handle hearing that.

Pieces of Eric's story start clicking into place in my head. He'd told me how hard it was, knowing there was always a "best friend" around Everly, someone from her past who lingered even when they were together. Was that best friend Jake? God. I should've let Jake warn me. I should've given him the chance to explain instead of walking into this blind.

Everly laughs. "You look like there's a lot going on in your head. I just wanted to apologize."

"What?" That breaks me out of my thoughts immediately.

Everly sighs. "I still feel really bad about what happened with Eric. I'm sure he told you things, but I'm hoping you'll want to know my side?"

I don't say anything, so she continues. "I really loved your brother, Jules. He is an amazing guy, and he was perfect. He just…"

She trails off, and I already know the answer, because Eric has said it many times. "He wasn't James."

She nods. "If I had ever thought James and I were getting back together, I never would've led Eric on like that. I really thought Eric and I could have an amazing life together, and we probably could have, but… I didn't think it was fair to him. That I still loved someone else…"

The way she says it, the look in her eyes… I believe her. My chest aches for her, because it's clear she's been carrying this weight for a long time. She isn't brushing it off or hiding behind excuses. She genuinely feels remorse for what happened between them. And I can see how much it still affects her.

I let out a deep breath. "I might have had a few harsh words and feelings about you back then, but I don't now. I can tell that you loved my brother, and you never meant to hurt him. Besides, I think he's met someone else who's great for him."

Her face lights up. "Really?"

I smile. "Yeah, really."

She lets out a breath as if she's been holding it since the day she broke up with him. The relief is noticeable. "I'm so happy to hear that. He deserves to be happy and to find love."

I nod.

"So we're good?" she asks, hopeful.

"Yeah, we're good."

"Great, because Jake is my best friend..." she says, then stops, watching me closely, waiting for my reaction.

"I..." The word catches in my throat, and the rest won't come. I don't know how to finish.

"Get it out now, Jules. Let's get past whatever it is."

I nod. "I was wondering... was Jake the best friend that would visit in college? Were you two... together?"

My heart sinks as I see Everly's guilty expression. Crap... I was right. What if... What if Jake isn't over her? What if this is another Everly-and-Eric mess all over again? Maybe he does love me, but what if he still loves her too? The idea twists in my stomach until I feel sick.

"I really think you should talk to Jake about that, but I'm going to tell you the one thing I am positive about. Okay?" she asks.

I nod, even though I don't know if I want to hear anything about her and Jake. "Jake is hopelessly in love with you. I can't speak to his feelings from before, only he can, but I can tell you that Jake never looked at me or any other girl the way he looks at you. He has never been so obsessed with anyone as he has you. You are who he loves, Jules."

Tears build in my eyes. I did not expect her to say any of that.

"Thank you," I say, and she smiles.

She gets up and reaches for a hug, but her stomach gets in the way. We both laugh a little awkwardly and end up in a side hug instead. It's clumsy, but somehow it feels real, like the first small step toward friendship.

"Sorry. I'm a big hugger, but I keep forgetting this thing is in the way."

I chuckle. "I can imagine it's a big adjustment. You're due soon?"

She nods. "I'm due at the end of July, but I have a feeling that she's going to come sooner."

"She?" I ask, and Everly nods.

"You're going to be a great mother, Everly."

"Thank you."

We walk back toward the gathering of friends, and I spot Jake on the couch, looking right at me. I can't help the smile that spreads across my face. Just seeing him there, relieved, worried, waiting for me, warms something inside me. A few seconds later, he's at my side. Everly winks at me as she heads back to James, sliding next to him while he rests an arm around her shoulder. They're undeniably cute together.

"Everything okay?" he asks, concerned.

I nod. "Yeah, I think so."

"What is it? Did Everly corner you? What happened?"

His concern makes me laugh, like he thinks Everly would sucker-punch me or something.

"What?" he asks, confused.

"Nothing. Yes, we talked, but it was good," I reassure him.

He nods and waits for me to take the lead, so I guide him back toward his friends. I know I'll have to talk to him about his feelings for Everly eventually, but not right now. Right now, I just want to be with him, to soak in this moment. Everly's right. He loves me. And I'm holding onto that. I push aside the thoughts of him still loving her, but they linger at the edges of my mind. If he does still love her… I don't know what I'll do…

CHAPTER THIRTY-THREE

JAKE

Jules has been off ever since she came back from talking to Everly. I don't know what was said, but I need to find out. She has been quiet for most of the ride home, staring at Stan. I know it's a lot, but I was hoping she'd adjust to my world quickly.

"So, tell me about these bodyguards everyone has on them," she breaks the silence.

I know she's avoiding what's really on her mind, but I'll bite... for now.

"They keep everyone safe." I chuckle.

She slaps my arm playfully. "No, seriously. Like, why do Everly and Amelia seem to have someone on them and watching their every move?"

I grow more serious as I answer but try to push away the thoughts that come with it. "When you have as much money as we do, it can be dangerous. Everly was kidnapped a bit ago, so

James is extra cautious. Bash feels the same way when it comes to Amelia, so he's not taking any chances."

She looks concerned before replying. "Was Everly okay? She seems okay..."

I nod. "Thankfully she was fine, but it doesn't make it any less scary."

She nods. "So... what does that mean for me?"

I pause for a moment before answering. "Well... at least for now, I'll definitely have Stan take you where you need to go, but I'll probably look into hiring someone for you once it's public we're together... if you still want that."

She doesn't respond, and my chest tightens. Why isn't she saying anything? Does she not want security? Or... is it something else? Is she unsure about us? Every second of silence feels like it's stretching into eternity, and I can feel the knot of worry twisting tighter in my gut.

Once we're inside my apartment, I press her against the wall, take her hands and hold them behind her back, slamming my mouth to hers. She moans, not pushing me away. Good.

When I pull back, I keep our bodies locked together. I'm not letting go, not until she tells me what's going on in that head of hers.

"Tell me what's wrong, Jules," I demand.

She rolls her eyes. "So you're going to trap me here against the wall until I tell you what's bothering me?"

I smirk. "I can stand here all day pressed against you."

She laughs. "So can I."

I kiss her again, just long enough to make her want me before pulling back again. "The faster we talk, the quicker we can move on."

She groans. "So you're ready to give in and sleep with me again?"

I grin. "You'll stay the night?"

Her expression hardens. "That depends... do you still love Everly?"

My heart skips a beat, and I step back, stunned by the question. "What?"

She frowns. "I know you were with her a while ago, but do you still love her?"

"She told you that?" I ask with a flicker of annoyance in my voice.

I had no idea what Everly said to Jules, but I never expected it to be about us, at least not like that. Why would she even bring that up? It's not something I would hide from Jules, but I also didn't plan on mentioning it. I wouldn't want to know about the guys she's slept with.

"So, you do still love her?" she asks, pulling away from me and the wall.

I grab her arm before she can get any further. "No, Jules. I don't love her. I mean as a friend, but not like that."

She doesn't believe me.

I run my hands through my hair. "I fell for her when we were in high school. She didn't love me back. We had a friends-with-benefits arrangement in college, but again, she didn't feel anything more for me than friendship."

"But you loved her."

I shrug my shoulders. "I thought I did, but now I'm not so sure."

"What do you mean?"

I laugh. "Is it not obvious? Damn, Jules. I fucking love you so much it hurts. When I think about the possibility that you could walk out of here and never come back, I feel like I'm drowning. Like the air gets ripped out of my lungs, and all that's left is the ache of you. So if you're going to leave, know that you're taking every last piece of me with you. I never felt that for her, and I'll never have anything left to give anyone else after you. It's you, Jules. You're it for me."

She throws herself at me, mouth pressing to mine with an urgency that makes my chest ache. I catch her easily, sliding my hands down her back to hold her close. Every inch of her fits perfectly against me, and I can feel how much she needs this too.

The kiss is fierce, desperate, and I don't hold back. Her lips, her hands, the way she presses into me, sets fire through my veins. I tilt my head, deepening the kiss, feeling her respond to me.

I pull back slightly, resting my forehead against hers. "You don't know how long I've been waiting for you, Jules. How much I need you."

She shivers at my words, hands clutching my shirt, and I tighten my grip around her waist, holding her like I'm afraid if

I let go, she'll disappear. Every brush of her lips, every press of her body, is electric, and I can't get enough.

I trail kisses along her jaw, down her neck, feeling her shiver against me. Her legs instinctively wrap around me, and I hold her tight, pressing her further against the wall, never wanting to let go.

"Jules," I murmur, voice low and husky, "I've never wanted anyone like this. Only you. Only us."

Her fingers dig into my back, pulling me closer, and I respond with every bit of control I can muster. The world falls away, the apartment, the wall, everything except her and me. This raw, undeniable pull between us.

I shift slightly, holding her against the wall, my hands sliding along her back, tracing the curves I've memorized without ever realizing it. Her body responds to mine, and it takes everything in me not to lose myself completely.

By the time we're moving toward the bedroom, we've forgotten everything else. Jackets, shoes, anything that slows us down, left behind, scattered, irrelevant. All that matters is the heat between us, the tension we can't hold back, the need that has been building far too long.

We stumble onto the bed, tangled together, pressed close enough to feel every gasp, every shiver, every pulse. I can't stop kissing her, hands sliding along her sides, holding her like I'll never let go. She responds in kind, her lips and hands and body matching my urgency, and it's perfect chaos.

"I need you, Jake," she says between kisses, and I know I can't deny her or myself any longer.

As I slide into her, she moans my name, and it takes every ounce of control to keep going and not let go just yet. We're lost together in that moment, every layer between us forgotten, every boundary gone. Nothing exists outside the walls of this apartment except us.

After finding our release together, we collapse onto the bed, limbs tangled, breathing heavy. I press my forehead to hers, feeling her chest rise and fall against mine, the warmth and rhythm grounding us.

As we lay in bed, wrapped in each other, I can't imagine my life without her. While she showed me what I needed to know, I need to hear it too.

"I need to know where we stand. I need to hear it," I say, holding my breath waiting for a response.

Jules rolls to her side, placing her hand on my face. "You're such an idiot, Jake, if you think I could live without you. I meant what I said before. I'm all in, no matter what. I don't care if you're a housekeeping manager, have no job, or are a billionaire. I'll go wherever you go, Jake. You kept me afloat when I was drowning and had nowhere to go in life. It's you and me against the world, always."

I choke back the lump rising in my throat at her words. Never in my life did I believe I'd be worthy of being loved like this, loved first, loved wholly. She's my world, and somehow, I'm hers. With her, I know we can survive anything.

She didn't just love me... she saved me. And maybe, in my own broken way, I saved her too. We're two souls who learned how to breathe again when we were both drowning. And for the first time, drowning didn't feel like the end. It felt like the beginning.

ALSO BY

Want more of Jake and Jules? Check out this bonus chapter to see a little into their future.

https://BookHip.com/MHHHWTV

If you haven't already, read the first four books in the series! Get a glimpse of Jake in high school and his past. Start the adventure with fALLINg into Summer.

If you'd like the inside scoop of upcoming books and releases, join my Facebook group:
www.facebook.com/groups/snchristensenreaders/

Follow me on TikTok
@authorsnchristensen

ACKNOWLEDGMENTS

There are so many people I want to thank for making it possible to write and share my stories with the world. With every book, I've been blessed to find people who stepped into my life at just the right moment, encouraging me in ways that shaped each story. I could easily fill twenty pages naming names, but please know this: whether you've supported me from the very beginning or encouraged me during this book in particular, I am deeply grateful for you. Each and every one of you has left a mark on my journey, and your encouragement means more than words can ever capture.

First, and foremost, to my Lord and Savior Jesus Christ who died for my sins so I may have eternal life. I give Him all the glory for blessing me with the gift of storytelling and the opportunity to share it with others.

To my biggest supporter since I was little, Aunt Karen. You have always believed in me, not just in my writing but in every dream I have ever chased. You spent countless hours editing my books, listening to my endless story ideas, and cheering me on. These books would hardly be readable without your time, patience, and love. With every new story, your excitement for my characters grows, and you remind me to keep going even when doubt creeps in. I could not ask for a greater champion.

To my husband, who read my stories as I wrote them, listened to every crazy idea that I had, and bounced back ideas. For taking care of the kids and allowing me to dedicate time to writing. For being understanding and taking on whatever role was needed when I was exhausted and stressed.

To Kim, for being my first official beta reader and going through each book with a fine-tooth comb to make sure the timeline is just right. For loving my characters and continuing to encourage me to write more even when I want to give up.

To Lexi, who has been part of my life for so many years but became an even bigger part of it just when I needed you most. You helped shape this book into what it is today with your encouragement and support. You took the time to read through every chapter, to talk through every detail, and to cheer me on at every step. Your friendship means more to me than I could ever put into words.

To Kelli, who was my first reader of these books and for being invested in the story and my characters. For understanding me and my anxiety by being there for me and texting as many times as I needed to support me.

To all my friends including Adrianna, Ashley, Wes, Sydney, Wendi, Jordin, and Kelly for believing in me and being excited for me to write these books. For continuing to support me through my writing journey and allowing me to share my excitement with you.

To my children, who have been patient with me and never once making me feel bad for spending time writing instead of time with you. To Amara, who constantly asked me how my book was coming along and being proud of me for being a writer. To Aiden, who graciously allowed me to go write and made me smile every time I finished for the day by being excited to see me again.

To my mother and father, who both believed in me from day one when I said I wanted to write a book. For always encouraging me to write the moment I said I wanted to be an author when I was little. For being excited and proud of me for my accomplishments.

To my ARC readers, for taking the time to read, review, and be honest about my books before it was released. For all the kind words and excitement for upcoming books and loving my characters the way I do.

And finally, to all my readers. I wrote these books because it was something that I'm passionate about. When I put them out there, I never expected anyone to actually read them. So, thank you for taking the time to read my stories and for getting invested in my characters. I can't wait to continue the stories of the characters and see where they take us.

S. N. Christensen

About the Author

S. N. Christensen lives in a town outside of Atlanta, Georgia. She holds a BA in English and MA in Secondary Education. From a young age, she has dreamed of being a writer. She loves writing in the fantasy, thriller, and romance genres.

When she is not writing or reading, she can be found teaching at her church preschool and serving at her church. When she is at home, she loves to spend time with her husband and two children playing games and crafting.

www.ingramcontent.com/pod-product-compliance
Lightning Source LLC
Chambersburg PA
CBHW020133310726
48970CB00006B/1855